He pulled the trigger. The finger drew back and I saw what happened next in the slowest motion possible. I saw the tiniest give when the trigger passed the point of no return and that little gear inside let the hammer smash down on the back of the casing of the shotgun shell. I swear that I saw the steel barrel of that shotgun swell a little near where the pellets began their supersonic journey to blow my head off, and I swear I could see that murderous bulge of lead death move down the barrel on its way towards me . . .

Want to know what happened next?

D0795335

GREG LYONS

BLOOMSBURY

LONDON BERLIN NEW YORK SYDNEY

Bloomsbury Publishing, London, Berlin, New York and Sydney

First published in Great Britain in March 2012 by Bloomsbury Publishing Plc
50 Bedford Square, London, WC1B 3DP

ISBN 978 1 4088 1674 5

1 3 5 7 9 10 8 6 4 2

Typeset by Hewer Text UK Ltd, Edinburgh
Printed in Great Britain by Clays Ltd, St Ives plc, Bungay, Suffolk

www.bloomsbury.com
www.averymcshane.blogspot.com
www.gleighlyons.com

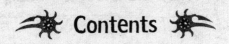# Contents

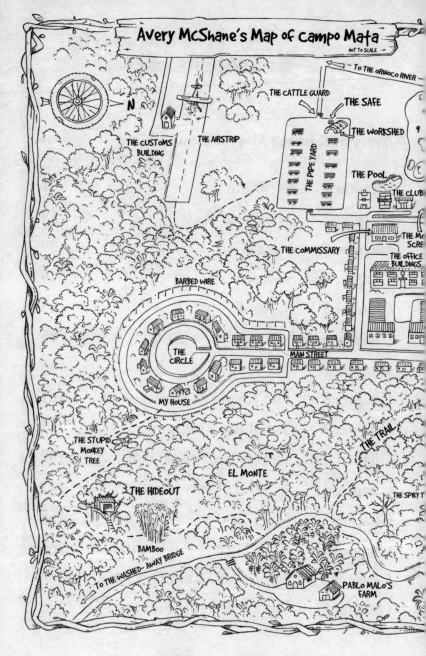

Avery McShane's Map of Campo Mata

NOT TO SCALE

To THE ORINOCO RIVER

N

THE CUSTOMS BUILDING

THE AIRSTRIP

THE CATTLE GUARD

THE SAFE

THE WORKSHED

THE PIPE YARD

THE POOL

THE CLUB

THE MOVIE SCREEN

THE COMMISSARY

THE OFFICE BUILDINGS

BARBED WIRE

THE CIRCLE

MAIN STREET

MY HOUSE

THE TRAIL

THE STUPID MONKEY TREE

THE HIDEOUT

EL MONTE

THE SPIKY TREE

BAMBOO

TO THE WASHED-AWAY BRIDGE

PABLO MALO'S FARM

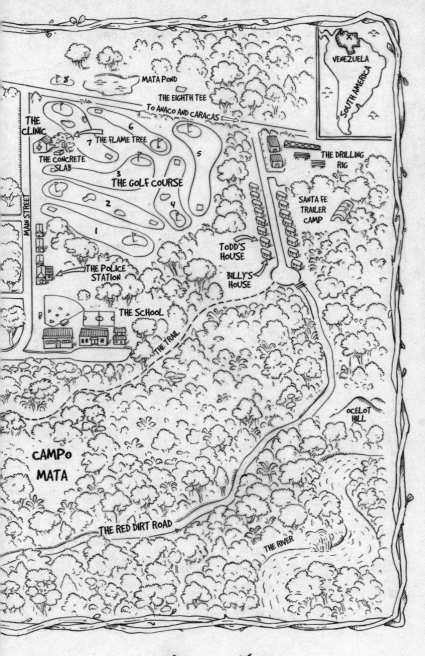

✺ Chapter 1 ✺

El Monte

It was a steamy hot day in the middle of nowhere in Venezuela. The sky was light blue, without a single cloud. I stood in front of the rusty barbed wire fence that circled Campo Mata, the place I called home. There was a gap in the fence where I had propped a board in between the lowest wires. It was my gateway into El Monte, the green, dark jungle that surrounded our camp. I hunched down and carefully stepped through the opening. Billy had ripped his shirt going through the gap last year and cut a gash in his back. His parents had made him get a tetanus shot. They said he'd end up getting lockjaw and have to eat

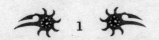

1

through a straw for the rest of his life if he didn't. I sure as heck wasn't going to get a shot, or lock-jaw. When I got through the gap I stood up to my full height of four feet, eleven and a half inches. I knew my exact height because I marked it on the wall next to the doorway in my bedroom. I had grown almost three inches in the last six months. I was sure I was almost a man now.

'Come on, Mati!' I called out. 'You can do it.'

Mati was my dog. My parents had named him Matisse after a famous artist from France. My mother was an artist, so I guess she was the one who came up with it. I don't remember because Mati was born about the same time I was. That was over twelve years ago, so I guess that made him almost ninety in dog years. He sure didn't act like a ninety-year-old. Mati jumped through the gap without losing any fur on the sharp barbs on the wires. He was an Australian Shepherd with one light blue eye and one black eye. He had a black coat with splotches of white on his hind end. It seemed to me that his tongue was always sticking out and he always had a happy smile.

We stood there on the other side of the fence looking at the tall wall of green trees in front of

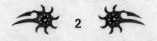

us. We were both excited. We had never gone into El Monte without having some sort of adventure.

We started down the short path through the tall dry grass that led into the tropical forest. It was going to take us about ten minutes to get to our hideout. Billy said he would be there waiting, and Todd said he'd try to make it too, but he was in trouble for fighting Alex, so I wasn't sure he'd be there. Mati and I stopped just before we reached the dark shadows of the trees. The huge trunks of the closest ones had long, hard spikes sticking out of them like big rose bush thorns. Getting pricked by one of those thorns really hurt. I couldn't tell you how many times it had happened to me. It would sting like a bee and it would keep stinging until my mom put some medicine and a Band-Aid on it. Mati somehow knew that too, because he never got poked by one of those spikes. I took a deep breath, big enough for the both of us, and then took that first heart-beating-hard step into El Monte.

The heat went away with the sunlight, but it seemed like the humidity went up a notch or two. I always sweated more in El Monte. Everything was wetter under the jungle canopy, even though

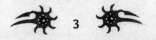

it hadn't rained for a few days. I guess the trees and plants had to sweat too. You could tell that Mati and I weren't the only ones to use the trail since it was bare dirt and it was packed down from all the animals that used it. The rest of the ground around the path was just tons of rotting leaves and moss and mushrooms and ferns everywhere. Everything was damp and you could see dewdrops on the mushroom caps, holding on for dear life. It smelled wet. I tried not to think of the different animals that used the path because I knew that most of them would love to catch me on it; at least they'd like it if Mati wasn't with me. He'd protect me for sure; always had before.

We were about halfway to the hideout when I heard the screeching of that stupid monkey. He'd seen me from way up in his tree and now he was raising a big fuss about me invading his territory. I didn't understand a thing he was saying, but I was pretty sure he was using all the curses and bad words he could think of. Couldn't be anything else from the nasty way he was yelling at me.

Mati started barking at the stupid monkey and they were raising quite a racket together. Monkey and I had crossed paths lots of times, so I knew

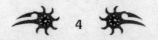

what was next. Sure enough, that skinny bag of bugs reached around to his behind and started throwing his poop down at us. I was ready for it and I had already ducked behind one of the spiky-trunked trees, but Mati wasn't so lucky. He caught one of those monkey poops right on his nose. He was trying to scrape that smelly stuff off with his front paws and, while he wasn't looking, he caught a few more chunks on his back before he gave up and started to run down the path to the hideout. I was right behind him.

Billy was already at the hideout when we came running down the path.

'Looks like you guys got caught in another poop storm,' laughed Billy.

I stopped running when I got to where Billy was standing on the outside of the ditch that we had dug around our hideout. I was breathing hard and now I was sweating like my dad did whenever he played a round of golf back at the camp.

'I hate that stupid monkey,' I said, gasping for air.

'Yeah, well, at least you don't have to go by Pablo Malo's farm to get here,' said Billy. 'Those gnarly dogs of his always come running after me

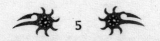

when I walk down that dang road by his banana trees.' He reached behind his back and pulled out his slingshot. 'Good thing I keep this in my pocket. Pegged that really mean one, Loca, smack-dab on her snout and she turned and ran.'

Billy Hale was my best friend in the world. Well, maybe Mati was my real best friend, but Billy was my best human friend, for sure. We'd both grown up in Campo Mata. Both of our fathers worked for oil companies. My dad was an engineer for one of the big oil companies, and Billy's dad worked for one of the oil service companies that drilled the oil wells for my dad's company. So my dad was kind of his boss, and I was kind of Billy's boss. This was mostly because he could never seem to beat me at anything unless I let him, like I had the other day when he challenged me to a wrestling match. I hoped he wouldn't try me right then because I was really tired from the escape from the stupid monkey. He didn't look like he would though.

Billy was shorter and thinner than me, which was saying something because I was pretty skinny. He was born in West Texas, like his parents, and

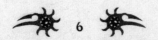

he had a really strong southern accent, like most of the kids in the oil camps. Almost all of them were born in Oklahoma or Louisiana or somewhere where there was lots of oil under the ground. I was born in California and moved to Campo Mata when I was six weeks old. Billy had bright red hair which his mom kept cut short. My hair was really blond and cut in a buzz cut too. Almost all of the boys in the camp had buzz cuts. Only one that didn't was Björn Sorensen, but he was from Europe and they seemed to do things differently over there. Billy always wore green jeans from Sears and red and white checked shirts with pearly buttons. I mostly wore Levi's blue jeans and a white T-shirt, which was never white for long. He wore cowboy boots and I wore black canvas sneakers. We both had cowboy hats but we almost never wore them. We'd stopped wearing our holsters with the six-shooters about a year ago. We were too old for that now. I had greenish eyes, and the moms in the camp always said things like 'Oh, isn't he sweet and so good-looking, like his dad' or 'I could just hug you all day'. Billy had eyes as blue as a gunfighter's, ears that stuck out from the side of his head like

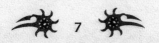

an elephant and an Adam's apple that made him look like he'd gotten a bone stuck in his throat. I never heard the moms gush over him much, except for his own mom, of course. So, other than the fact that we were both skinny as rails, we were pretty much opposites in most ways.

Billy and I looked at each other and then turned our eyes to the huge trunk of the mango tree about twenty metres away. We both started running for it at the same time.

'Last one's a rotten egg,' I yelled.

'You already stink,' yelled Billy.

I beat him by a step, but I still had to push him away from the wooden plank steps that we had nailed to the trunk to get to our hideout high in the thick branches of the mango tree. He fell down on his rump and I started to climb.

'You're such a jerk, Avery,' he grumbled as he got to his feet, swatting the muddy leaves from his rump. 'Who made you the boss?'

I was already halfway up the trunk when I stopped to look down at him. He always tried to make me feel guilty when I beat him at something, and I almost always did feel guilty. I guess it's how good friends feel when that happens.

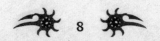

'Aw, come on, Billy,' I replied. 'Don't be a sore loser. You should be used to it by now.'

I felt bad as soon as I said it. It just wasn't a nice thing to say, especially to my best friend. I tried to think of something that would make him feel better and keep him from being grumpy the rest of the day.

'It wasn't fair,' I said. 'I was already warmed up running from that stupid monkey and you weren't ready. I think we tied anyway. I mean, I had to push you out of the way, didn't I?'

Billy was no fool. He knew that I'd out-raced him, but all he needed was something to hang his hat on, and that was good enough for him.

'Yeah, I guess so,' he said. 'Besides, I think you got the jump on me.'

Billy started up the ladder about the time I made it into the hideout. It was the most special place in the world. No girls had ever been there or would ever be there. They wouldn't dare. It was a tree house made out of pine boards from the pipe yard in the camp. My dad built most of it the summer before. He and I had carried the long wooden boards down the path past the stupid monkey until we had a big pile of them

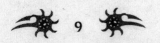

underneath the mango tree. He brought a handsaw, a hammer and lots of nails. On the first day he finished the steps and the floor. The next day, all by himself, my dad dragged lots of sheets of rusted and used tin roofing through the jungle and made a roof for our tree house. Billy and I, with a little help from Todd (when he wasn't grounded), built up the walls of our hideout. It took a long time and it seemed like years, but it was probably only a week or two. So the floor was really nice and flat, and didn't have any cracks in it. And the roof never leaked when the rains came. The walls that Billy and I built by ourselves weren't so good, but that didn't matter to us. We painted the whole tree house in army green so that our enemies, especially the girls, couldn't see it from below. It had worked so far.

Billy's head poked up through the opening in the floor of our hideout and he carefully looked around before climbing all the way in. He did that every time we climbed up to the tree house, ever since last year when we had been close to finishing the walls and he had come face-to-face with the iguana. Billy had beaten me to the steps that day, and he was still laughing and calling me a 'rotten egg' when he poked his head through the opening in the floor and came nose-to-nose with the iguana. From that distance it must have looked more like Godzilla. All I remember was a girly high-pitched scream and a hard thud as Billy landed on the ground next to me. He ended up breaking his arm and got to wear a cast. He still has that cast and it has all of the names of our classmates on it. I drew a picture of Godzilla on it.

Our hideout was roomy. We could stand up straight inside without banging our heads on the tin roof and it was about five or six paces across. We kept all kinds of stuff in there. Our old holsters with the cap-gun pistols were hanging from nails on the far wall. Even though we didn't wear them any more we kept them there in case some girls showed up and we had to shoot them. All along the walls were our most prized possessions. Our comic book collections were stacked up high on the left wall. Billy was a fan of the *Iron Man* comics, while I liked *Thor*. We both knew that Thor could use his hammer to pound Iron Man's metal suit to a pulp, but I never made a big deal of it. I had about ten of my favourite Louis L'Amour western paperback novels next to my

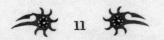

pile of comics, and Billy had his seven or eight Max Brand westerns next to his. We were big fans of westerns. I was pretty sure that Billy would have been a gunfighter like one of his Max Brand heroes, if he'd been born about a hundred years ago.

Jam jars and Mason jars full of all kinds of weird things that we had found in El Monte were stacked up along the right wall, just underneath the only window in our hideout. The most special of those weird things was the worm snake.

A few months ago, when we were digging the moat around the trunk of our mango tree, Billy let out one of his scaredy, girly screams, dropped his shovel and ran away really fast. Not knowing why he skittered away so suddenly I ran after him, and away from whatever it was.

'What the heck's going on?' I yelled when I caught up to him.

'I dug up a snake!' he screamed back. He was still running and looking back at the half dug ditch. His eyes were wide with terror. They were pretty much the same eyes he'd had when he met up with Godzilla.

'A snake buried in the dirt?' I replied. We had

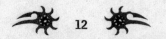

stopped running. 'Snakes don't dig holes in the ground. Come on, let's see what it is.'

We worked our way back to the ditch, hiding behind tree trunks like soldiers sneaking up on an enemy camp. When we reached the big mound of dirt that we had piled up on the outside of the moat, we stopped and looked over it. There it was, halfway out of a hole in the side of the ditch, right next to the shovel that Billy had dropped. The part that stuck out was about half a metre long and thick as a garden hose. It was a sickly whitish colour and it was wriggling around slowly.

'That's not a snake,' I said. 'That's a worm.'

'Is not,' replied Billy. 'No such thing as a worm a metre long.'

I walked around the pile of dirt and into the freshly dug out ditch. I picked up Billy's shovel and prodded the wriggling worm snake thing. When I did that it started to move into its tunnel, so I dropped the shovel and grabbed it by its tail or head or whatever that end of it was. Billy almost had a heart attack.

'Let go of it,' he cried. 'It's gonna come out and bite you, and you'll have to go to the clinic to get all those anti-venom shots like Eric.'

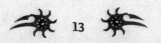

'Nah . . . it's a worm all right,' I replied, pulling on it. 'I need some help.'

Billy wasn't having any of it and he stayed put behind the protection of the dirt pile as if he thought the critter might blow up like a grenade or something.

I was starting to win the tug of war with the worm. Little by little it started to come out of the worm hole. I was careful to not pull too hard. I didn't want to snap it in two and have worm guts and juice flying all over the place. I was just starting to wonder how long the thing was when the rest of it finally popped out and I almost fell over on my butt. I dropped it on the ground and it thrashed around in the way that normal earthworms do when you dig them up to put on a fish hook; only this one would need a hook the size of an anchor to use as bait.

'See?' I said triumphantly. 'No eyes, no mouth, no fangs – not even any rattles or scales. It's a worm, that's all.'

We put that worm in the biggest glass jar we had, filled it up with dirt and then poked some holes in the cap so it could breathe. That was the coolest thing in our jar collection of bugs and fish.

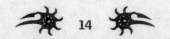

We also had jars with piranhas that we'd caught in the river (with smaller worms) and monster rhinoceros beetles. We even had one full of machacas, which is what we called the huge ants with big pincers that lived everywhere around Campo Mata. Those machacas could cut the leaves off a whole tree in one day and march away along the ant highways that they'd made on the ground to their volcano mounds. The ant highways were all over the place and they always led to one of the huge mounds of dirt that they'd built up. We didn't mess with those customers too much. Rumour had it that they could clean the meat off the bones of a sleeping person faster than a pack of piranhas.

We also had shoeboxes full of other bugs; neat ones like centipedes, millipedes, machaca queen ants (with their wings still on them) and tons of butterflies and moths. All of them were much bigger and brighter than the kinds you find back in the States. What we didn't have were snakes. We'd collected some snakeskins, but Billy and I didn't get near live snakes. They scared the heck out of both of us.

We were standing at the window of our tree

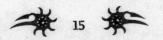

house when Todd came crashing through the bamboo thicket behind our hideout, down the same path that Billy always took. We had heard him coming for quite a while, mostly because he had been yelling our names the whole time.

'Avery . . . Billy,' he yelled between big gulps of air. 'Guys, there's a dead body on the slab behind the clinic! We gotta go and see it.'

Todd Shanker was a lot bigger than Billy and me. Not just taller, but he weighed more and he was really strong. But he was also dumber than a doornail or, as my dad once said, 'Todd's not the sharpest tool in the shed, that's for sure'. I always wondered how he could have such a big head and such a tiny brain. It must have rattled around in there. He had blond hair like me, and it was buzz cut too. He had brown eyes and they were really close together, like a weasel's. He had a tiny nose that didn't do a good job of hiding the holes of his nostrils, which made it too easy to see the crusty chunks of snot he always had up there. A couple of years ago I caught him picking at them and eating them. He got really mad at me when he realised I had seen him. If he didn't know how to handle an awkward situation he would just beat you up. It made him feel better somehow, I don't know why. He was wearing a pair of cut-off jeans, dirty sneakers and a black cotton shirt with a little green alligator sewn on to it just above where your heart should be. He didn't eat snot any more, but he also never wiped away the two trails that seemed to always leak down from his nose to his upper lip. Todd was my second best friend; third if you counted Mati.

Billy and I got on our hands and knees and looked down through the opening of our hideout at Todd. He looked up and waved at us to come down.

'I heard it from my brother,' he said, still trying to catch his breath. 'There's some local guy lying dead on the concrete slab at the back of the clinic. He said that there's blood and guts and that it's really gross. We gotta go and see it.'

I had seen one other dead body on that concrete slab before. He had been driving one of the big eighteen-wheelers hauling drill pipe to one of the rigs in the oil field when he lost control and crashed. The pipe had come smashing through the cab of the truck and went right through him too. That one was definitely gross. I doubted that

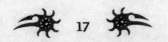

this one would be as gross, but I knew that we just had to go and find out.

'You sure?' I asked. 'I don't want to go all the way home to get my bike and pedal all the way across the camp and find out that your big brother was just pulling your leg all along.'

'No, it's real all right,' replied Todd excitedly. 'Come on, let's go.'

✹ Chapter 2 ✹

The Dead Body

Stupid Monkey only got out a couple of screams this time as Mati and I ran past his tree. He didn't even have time to squish out a couple of poops to throw at us. I squeezed through the barbed wire fence surrounding El Monte and started running across the mowed grass field to my house. Mati was already in the shade under the carport when I got there. My super special BMX dirt jumper bike was leaning up against one of the metal poles that held up the open carport. I called my bike Mamba since it was painted black, but mostly because it was such a cool name. My dad's company car wasn't there, so I knew he wasn't back for lunch yet. I jumped on my bike and started pedalling like crazy down our gravel drive-way. Our maid, Nelly, must have seen me because she showed up at the front door with a broom in her hand.

'*Querido*, where are you going?' she asked in Spanish.

'To the clubhouse,' I yelled back over my shoulder.

I had lied. There was no way she'd let me go to the clinic to see a dead body. I aimed the bike for a small dirt jump that I'd built off to the side of the driveway. I always went for it when I left the house and, since Nelly was watching, I decided to show off. I hit the jump, flew into the air, and then I took both feet off the pedals and stuck my legs out. My feet were back on the pedals when I landed.

'No footer,' I yelled back to Nelly after I'd landed.

I always told her the name of each trick I did when she was watching.

'*Fantástico*,' she yelled back.

I could do way neater things on the humongous jumps that Billy and I had built at the foot of

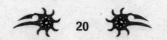

Ocelot Hill. I practised on them so much that I was easily the best dirt jumper around, and everyone knew that I was the only rider in Campo Mata to safely land a backflip.

The playing cards that I had clamped down on the forks of the bike with clothespins started to clack faster and louder as the bike picked up speed. I pushed the lever of the round metal ringer on the handlebar with my thumb again and again, ringing it non-stop. I was on official business, so I was making it clear to everybody who could hear me. I was really moving, even though I had to dodge lots of squashed and flattened toads that had been run over by cars. They were slick as banana peels just after they'd been smushed by a car tyre, so I didn't want to slip on one of them and end up in the clinic with a big scrape, or worse. Most of the toad-frisbees though were all dry and hard from being in the sun for days. I whooshed past the Fultons' house and down the main street of the camp. I was the only one on the road. Since it wasn't lunchtime yet the company cars were all in the parking lot of my dad's office building. I saw them there when I went past it. My dad's white Ford pick-up truck

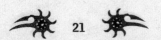

was in his parking space in front of the little sign that said, *Reserved for Chief Engineer*. I was not far from the clinic now.

I saw the tall whitewashed concrete wall of our outdoor movie screen up ahead of me, and the buildings of the club. We had a tennis court, a bowling alley and a restaurant in there. My dad told me that every piece of the alley and the court was made in the States, so they were like ones that you'd see there. At least I thought so. I wasn't positive because I'd never seen any others. I passed the road to the commissary, which was where our parents bought groceries and stuff.

I was practically flying down the road; faster than anyone else on a dirt bike could go. By now the ninth green of our golf course was to my left and I saw the little red flag with the number of the green on it flapping in the hot breeze. Just up ahead, on the right side of the road, was the white one-storey building with the big red cross painted on the side – the clinic.

Way over to the right in the distance, I could see Billy and Todd on their BMXs racing across the golf course fairways, trying to reach the dead man before me, but there was no way they would.

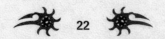

They still had to cross two more fairways and I was moving at top speed on the asphalt street. I jumped Mamba over the cement sidewalk and across the grass, making a beeline for the concrete slab. Just before I went around the corner of the building, I saw a Venezuelan police car in the parking lot in front of the clinic. I sure hoped that the local fuzz weren't already standing next to the body. Luckily they weren't.

I saw the outline of the dead guy on top of the concrete table. There was a white sheet pulled over the body, but I could see a couple of red spots where blood had seeped through. I jumped off my bike and leaned it against the trunk of the huge flame tree that shaded the whole area behind the clinic. It was the biggest tree in the camp and it was blooming with those bunches of super bright red flowers that covered all of the branches. There were flowers all over the ground, and there were even a few of them that had landed on the white sheet on top of the dead guy. It seemed like a massacre had happened with the body, the bloody sheet and all the red flowers on the ground.

Billy and Todd came flying into the shade of

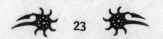

23

the flame tree and slammed on their brakes at the same time that they pushed their back tyres to the side. They kicked up a big wave of dirt and grass that covered me from head to foot. They laughed at me as they leaned their bikes against the trunk of the tree, while I spat out the pieces of grit that had gotten into my mouth.

'Very funny, guys,' I grumbled as I continued to dig out chunks of grass and dirt from under my T-shirt. I would have done the same thing to them if I'd had the chance.

'I can see some blood on the sheet,' said Billy in a whisper. It was as if he thought he'd wake the man up from the dead if he spoke in a louder voice.

'How'd he die, Todd?' I asked.

'Don't know,' he replied. 'But it doesn't look like enough blood to be from some really gross accident. Let's look.'

We approached the body on the cement slab until we were all three standing next to the end where the head was.

'Go ahead, Avery,' said Billy in his low voice. 'Pull the sheet back.'

'You do it,' I replied.

'No way,' whispered Billy.

We both looked at Todd.

'Hey, I'm the one who told you about the body,' said Todd as he shook his head from side to side. 'One of you's gotta do it.'

'All right . . . rock, paper, scissors,' I said, turning to Billy.

We faced each other with our hands out.

'One, two, three . . .'

My right fist pounded into the palm of my left hand at the same time that Billy's flat hands slapped together.

'Dang it,' I muttered. Paper beats rock every time.

I reached out and grabbed the edge of the sheet with my forefinger and thumb, like I was about to pick a fly out of my soup. My heart started to beat fast again. I pulled the sheet down until the dead guy's face was showing. Billy and Todd were bending over the body with their hands on their knees.

His dark brown eyes were still open, which scared the holy beejeebies out of us. I let the sheet fall over the dead guy's neck and took a quick step back. Billy and Todd were right there

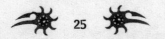

with me. His mouth was open too. It looked like he had been surprised when he met his maker. The guy was kind of youngish, maybe about twenty years old. He had a nice-looking face. It was the kind of face with long Latin eyelashes and bright white teeth that the young maids in camp would have liked. His long black hair was pulled back tight in a ponytail and I could see the impression of the ring of a hat. I had seen that a lot whenever one of the local gauchos took his cowboy hat off before coming into a room. Normally dead men's hats would be placed over their faces or on their chests when they laid out a body – at least that's what they did in western novels – but this guy's was nowhere to be seen. So far we hadn't seen where the blood had come from.

'Keep going, Avery,' whispered Billy.

I stepped back to where I was before and reached out again to the sheet. This time I grabbed it with all of my fingers and ripped the sheet off the body. We stared at the wounds while the sheet fell to the ground. He had been shot twice, right in the middle of his chest. There wasn't much blood on the blue denim shirt; just two half-dollar-sized splotches with dark holes in the middle where the bullets had gone in. He was wearing blue jeans, like the ones I was wearing. He had a thick leather belt with a huge silver buckle. The belt buckle had the image of a bucking bronco etched into it. The guy had been a gaucho – a real cowboy – that much was clear. He wore pointy-toed cowboy boots with silver tips that matched the belt buckle. He didn't have spurs on, but I could see the rub marks in the heel of his boots which meant that he had worn them when he was on his horse. He must have looked pretty grand up there on his horse when he was alive. I'm not sure why – I didn't know him – but I felt sad to see him like that.

'*Oye, muchachos*,' came a loud yell from behind us. '*Vete* . . . get away from there!'

All three of us whirled around to see Capitán Gómez running out of the back screen door of the clinic. He was wearing his khaki uniform and the tall knee-high black leather boots that he always wore around the camp. His eyes were hidden by his reflective aviator glasses, but we could see the angry expression on the rest of his face. His lips were now pulled tight in determination underneath his pencil-thin moustache. Without a word

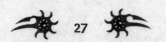

all three of us ran to our bikes, hopped on them and took off in three different directions. This was how we always did it. We always split up in opposite directions to confuse our enemies, and then we would get back together at the hideout. I looked back over my shoulder to see what Gómez was up to. He had stopped running and was just standing there with his hands on his hips, next to the two guns that he kept in the holsters at each side. He looked like an old western gunfighter, only without the cowboy hat. Just before I made it out of sight around the corner of the clinic, I saw his mouth turn into a smile and I could swear I heard him chuckle. I wasn't going back to find out.

✹ Chapter 3 ✹

Mata Pond

'The man's name was Gustavo Muñoz,' said my dad without looking up. He was standing behind the bamboo bar stand in the atrium of our house, opening a couple of bottles of beer. He handed one of the perspiring bottles to Mr Slater, who was sitting on one of the matching stools on the other side of the bar.

'Gómez said he was murdered,' replied Mr Slater. 'Young guy . . . I remember him coming into the clubhouse every now and then for a beer. Seemed like a nice guy.'

Mr Slater was a huge, tall man. He was the biggest man I had ever seen, but he was also just

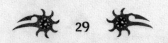

about the nicest guy I had ever met. He was like a big, gentle bear and he always seemed to have some time for me, which was more than I could say about most of the adults in Campo Mata. The only times I ever saw him get mad were when I caddied for Dad on the golf course and he'd hit a bad shot. His face would get all red and he'd usually pound his club on the ground or sometimes even throw it into the air. One time he threw his club further than his golf ball went. Mr Fulton, who was the captain of the golf club, had even taken to collecting all of Mr Slater's busted clubs and had put them up on the wall of the clubhouse bar. Main reason he got so mad was that he never could beat my dad at golf even though it seemed like they played almost every day. My dad was the camp champion, and I was pretty good too. I had been playing golf ever since my dad gave me my first set of clubs on my fifth birthday.

'Good-looking kid like that probably got on the wrong side of some girl's boyfriend,' added my dad. 'Local boys always seem to get a little hot-headed about that kind of thing.'

Mr Slater took a big swig of his beer and then

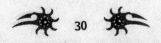

grabbed a handful of cashew nuts from the bowl in front of him. We had picked the nuts from the cashew trees in the backyard last weekend and then roasted them over the grills of the big barbecue pit. Most of the families in Campo Mata had come over for the roasting party.

I could see the bamboo bar through the open doorway from where I was sitting on the kitchen counter. Nelly had just fried up some *arepas* with cheese in the middle for us to snack on. *Arepas* were like really thick corn tortillas and pretty much the best thing ever invented in Venezuela. I had stolen one from the pile next to the frying pan when she wasn't looking. Of course, she knew that I'd be stealing one, just like I did every day. She even turned her back on purpose for me to grab the *arepa*. It was delicious; my favourite food in the whole world. Just like my dad and Mr Slater, I had a sweating bottle of my favourite drink next to me too, only my favourite drink was orange Fanta. I tried a sip of beer one time about a year ago and almost threw up on the spot. I did throw up a bit later when I saw the cigarette butt in the bottom of the glass.

I could smell the familiar stinky odour of my

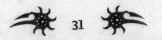

dad's cigar drifting into the kitchen. The cigar smoke smell almost totally covered up the smell of Mr Slater's cigarette. I guess it was an oilfield thing because it seemed like most of the adults in camp smoked something and drank something with alcohol in it, mostly cold beer. I guess because it was always hot in Campo Mata.

I was still waiting for Nelly to act like she was mad at me for stealing the *arepa*, but she hadn't said a word. I pivoted my butt on the yellow Formica counter and looked at her as she kept on frying. She was looking down at what she was doing and her long black hair covered her face, so I couldn't see her expression, but I knew something was wrong. She was just sort of pushing the *arepas* around in the pan with the wooden spatula and I could see that they were burning. Nelly never burned anything.

'*Qué pasa*, Nelly?' I asked.

'*Nada . . . no te preocupes,*' she replied in a whisper without looking up.

'*Las arepas estan quemando,*' I said, pointing at the smoking pan.

Nelly turned off the burner, picked up the frying pan and dumped it in the sink. She turned

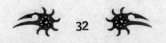

on the faucet and the water hissed into a cloud of greasy steam. Then, she turned off the water, wiped her hands on her white apron and walked out of the kitchen in the direction of her room at the back of our house. She disappeared into her room and I heard the door close with a click.

What the heck? I could swear that she was crying. I just didn't get adults sometimes. Only time I would cry is if I got hurt from falling off my bike, or when my mom put some super stingy medicine on a cut. But adults would sometimes cry for no reason at all that I could see. My mom would even cry when she was happy, like the time my dad gave her a pearl necklace. I couldn't be totally sure, but I think I saw a tear in my dad's eyes too. Adults are so weird sometimes.

Mr Slater sometimes came over to our place for a drink after a weekend round of golf with my dad. To the adults, this was just another weekend, but for me it was the start of a three-month-long weekend. School had just let out for summer break. Some of my friends had already gone back to the States, but most of them would be staying in Campo Mata for the break like me. It was my

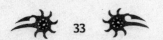

dad's turn to stay for the summer in Venezuela to make sure that the wells were drilled and the oil kept flowing out of the ground.

Last summer we had gone back to California on vacation. We stayed with my mom's parents and got to go to Disneyland. I liked a lot of things about the States, especially Disneyland and most especially Peter Pan's Magic Ride. It was so cool to sit in that magic ship flying over London at night time. There were lots of other things I liked too. Like A & W root beer and burgers, Orange Julius and all of the cool cars. My favourite car was a Ford Bronco because it was named after the kind of horse cowboys ride and also because it was really good off-road, like my BMX.

There were lots of things I didn't like about the States too. For starters there were too many buildings and freeways, and everybody seemed to be way busier and more stressed out than folks around here. And most of the time, when I told people in the States that I lived in Venezuela, they didn't ever seem to know where that was. They'd say things like 'Is that in Mexico?' or 'What language do they speak there?' It made me wonder if they'd ever looked at a map of the world.

I jumped down from the kitchen counter and walked into the atrium with my Fanta in my hand. I was going to mosey up to the bar and join my dad and Mr Slater. I was almost an adult now, so I didn't see a problem.

'Avery, we're having an adult conversation right now,' said my dad. 'You run along now, OK? Maybe go to the club and hit a practice ball or two for the junior tournament next Saturday.'

'Aww, I wanted to hear more about the dead guy,' I moaned.

'That's exactly why I want you to vamoose,' replied my dad with that fake mean look on his face. 'You keep your nose out of this, you hear me?'

'I promise. Cross my heart and hope to die.'

I didn't go straight to the golf club. I went to Billy's house first. It was actually a big trailer home. The families whose parents worked for the service companies lived in a trailer park on the east side of Campo Mata. My dad said they lived in them

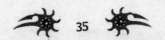

because the service companies moved around a lot after they finished their jobs for each oil company. It was easier to hook up the trailers and take them to a new job than it was to build brick houses like ours each time.

I hauled down the gravel road on Mamba, past Todd's white and pink trailer, and skidded to a dusty stop in front of Billy's light blue trailer next door. I left my bike on the tiny grass lawn. I could hear the noise of all of the air conditioners in the trailer park, sounding like millions of hornets buzzing around their nests. I never had to knock on the door at the Hales' trailer, so I just opened it and let myself in. As usual it was freezing cold. I'm not sure why they even had a fridge. It was cold enough in there to keep fish fresh for a year. I didn't see Billy's mom around, but I knew he was home because I had seen his old rusted dirt bike outside and his boots were on the front door steps. I walked on my tiptoes on the orange shag rug that covered the floor of the narrow hallway to his room at the back of the trailer. His door was closed, but I knew that he wasn't asleep. It was almost two o'clock and though Billy always slept in late, I figured he'd be awake by now. I got to the door and put my ear to it to hear what he was up to, but I didn't hear anything going on inside the room. My ear almost froze to the metal door. If I'd put my tongue on it, I'd probably have gotten it stuck, like sometimes happens with ice cubes. I grabbed the little round door handle and turned it slowly so as to not make a sound. I took a deep breath and then burst into the room yelling at the top of my lungs.

'Banshee come to get ya!' I screamed.

Billy was in the top bunk reading a comic book. He almost jumped out of his skin and banged his head on the ceiling just above him. I laughed so hard I started coughing.

'Oww! Avery, dang it,' he moaned, rubbing the top of his bumped head. 'Why can't you just knock?'

'That wouldn't be any fun, would it?' I replied. 'Whatcha doin'?'

Billy threw his comic book at me, but it missed. He was sitting cross-legged in his Spiderman underwear and nothing else.

'None of your business.'

I picked up the comic, a little surprised to see Thor on the cover.

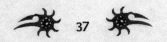

'So you've finally come around. Admit it, Thor's greater than Iron Man,' I said in my most taunting manner.

'No way, Jose,' he cried. 'Thor can't fly as fast as Iron Man and besides, Iron Man's a lot smarter.'

'Yeah, whatever. Wanna come and hit some balls?'

'Sure, but I promised Mom I'd take a shower and brush my teeth,' replied Billy as he jumped down from the bunk. 'I'd better at least turn on the water and get the toothbrush wet so she'll think I did.'

While Billy went down the hall to try to fool his mom, I went over to the lower bunk and sat down. There was a rolled-up copy of yesterday's newspaper with a chewed-up pencil on top of it. I opened up the paper and glanced at the front page. Normally I would just go to the sports section to see how my favourite soccer teams had done over the weekend, but when I saw a photo of the face of the dead guy that we had seen on the concrete slab, I stopped to read the article. I guess Billy had already read it because the article had been circled with a pencil.

The body of Gustavo Muñoz was discovered yester-day morning at the end of the airstrip in Campo Mata. It was discovered by the pilot of a single engine Cessna loaded with supplies for the local commis-sary. He told police that he had seen the body as he approached the landing strip and reported it to the police shortly after landing.

The Capitán of Police, Aurelio Gómez, confirmed the discovery. Señor Muñoz was shot twice in the chest with bullets from a .45 calibre pistol. Capitán Gómez estimated that the time of death was within twenty-four hours of the discovery and has launched an official investigation. A reward of five thousand bolivars has been offered by the family of the deceased for any information leading to the arrest of the perpetrators. Anyone with information is asked to contact Capitán Gómez.

Billy came back into the room dressed in his green jeans and checked shirt. His hair wasn't even the least bit wet and I didn't smell any mint on his breath. He sat down next to me and pulled on the same holey socks he had taken off and thrown on the floor last night.

'Looks like it was no hunting accident, huh?' said Billy, looking at his socks.

'Yeah, my dad and Mr Slater were talking about it today,' I replied, scratching my head. 'They say the guy was murdered and they think it probably had something to do with a jealous boyfriend or something like that. Anyway, it's none of our business. You ready?'

'Yep.'

When we got to the eighth hole, the one where you had to hit the ball over Mata Pond, we stripped down to our underwear for a quick swim. It wasn't anything new. We always took a dip in the pond when we got there. The pond wasn't very big, but it was bigger than the pool at the club and there weren't ever any girls hanging around it, like at the pool. It was ringed with tall reeds and cat's tails. Since it was between the tee and the green it was always full of golf balls that hadn't made it across. I had lost a bunch in it myself, but I had found lots more in there than I had lost. At the beginning of every summer Billy and I would cut a path through the reeds to get to the cool clear water in the middle. That's why we had brought our machetes in our golf bags on this round. It was our first round of the summer. Since those machetes were so heavy, we had borrowed our dads' pull carts instead of carrying the golf bags on our backs like we normally did.

So there we were. Two skinny pale kids in comic book underwear, each hanging on to huge machetes. We started hacking our way through the reeds, like berserk Vikings tearing through a helpless army. We were sweating pretty good by the time we broke through to the open water. We stabbed the pointed ends of our machetes into the mud in the shallow water next to us and swam out to the middle of the pond. We floated on our backs in the cool water, watching the clouds drift by above.

'That one looks like a capybara,' I said, pointing up.

'Yeah, I see it,' replied Billy. 'That one over there looks like a pig . . . see the snout?'

'Sure do.'

We messed around for a little while longer before we decided to get down to business.

'Let's find some golf balls.'

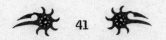

We dived down at the same time and started looking for the white treasures. My dad paid us a US quarter for each golf ball we found in good condition, and a dime for the ones with cuts in them. It was our main source of spending money, which went mostly on ham and cheese sandwiches and Fanta at the clubhouse. Even so, we'd managed to save about forty dollars. We kept the money in our secret hiding place in the pipe yard. We did pretty good that day. When our underwear was chock-full of golf balls we swam back to the path through the reeds, picked up our machetes and walked out of the thicket.

We almost walked straight into them – Scott Barnett and Chris Sanders, the meanest bullies in the camp. When they saw us come out of the reeds, with our comic book underwear full of golf balls and our machetes half as big as us, they doubled over laughing. Scott pointed at me and looked over at Chris.

'Look at these weirdos,' he said with a not so nice smile. 'You guys been laying eggs?'

I hated these guys. They were fourteen years old and a lot bigger than Billy and me. Their parents had moved to Campo Mata from Dallas a

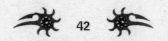

42

year or so back. They had been best friends before they moved here. Their parents told my parents that they were really mad about leaving the big city for Campo Mata and that was why they were so mean to everybody. I didn't buy it. I think they were born mean and would always be that way. I was thinking of something mean myself; at least I was thinking of something mean to say.

'Leave us alone,' I said. 'We're just finding golf balls.'

It was a pretty lame thing to say, especially because I had wanted to say something mean.

'Da widdo boys wookin' fo' balls?' laughed Chris.

These guys really got under my skin.

'Better than just walking around picking our noses, like you two do all the time,' I replied.

The taunting smiles disappeared from their faces and were replaced by nasty looks.

'Give us the golf balls or we'll just have to kick your butts,' growled Scott. 'We'll probably kick your butts anyway.'

Billy hadn't said a word, hadn't even moved a muscle. He might have been just a little whip of a kid, but he had an ornery streak in him. As for me,

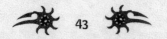

43

I never backed down from anything. I had Thor and even Iron Man to answer to. I wasn't going to let them down; not now, not ever. I lifted my machete and pointed it at the two bullies. Out of the corner of my eye I saw Billy's machete come up too.

'You want 'em? Come and get 'em,' said Billy in his best West Texas gunslinger drawl.

The two bullies just stood there staring at us. They couldn't believe it.

'You wouldn't dare,' spat Chris.

'Try us,' replied Billy in that same slow drawl.

I saw a car slowly pull off on to the shoulder of the main road directly behind the bullies. I recognised Capitán Gómez's police car and saw him sitting behind the steering wheel looking at us. Chris and Scott heard the crunching of the gravel under the tyres and turned around to look. They waved politely at the police chief and then turned back to face us.

'It ain't over,' whispered Scott. 'Not by a long shot.'

They turned away from us, waved once more at Gómez and began walking towards the eighth green.

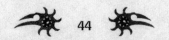

I looked back at the police chief. It was hard to see his face through the reflection of the sunlight on the windshield of his car, but I thought I saw a smile on the lips beneath the pencil-thin moustache. He put the car into gear and drove off in the direction of the clinic.

Chapter 4

Silver Spurs

It was Saturday, the day we always got together at the hideout at the stroke of noon. We called ourselves the Machacas because we made all kinds of paths through El Monte, like those big ants did. We also liked the idea of being fierce and super protective of our hideout, just like the ants were when someone messed up their volcano mounds. My dad got rid of the ants by pouring gasoline into the hole at the top of each mound and then tossing a burning match into it. Huge flames would shoot straight up out of the tops of each of the mounds, like real live erupting volcanoes. It was especially cool when he did that at night.

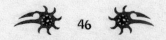

I was always the first to the hideout on Saturdays. Since I was the President of the Machacas, I had to make sure that the hideout was ready for the meeting. First thing I did before climbing up the tree was to go around to each of the paths that led to the tree house and make sure that no one had invaded our territory. We had strung up black sewing thread across the six different paths that we had made leading to the hideout. We usually tied the thread to a branch or tree trunk next to the path and then stretched it across to another branch. One of the knots was always really loose so that the invader wouldn't know they had triggered the alarm. We called them 'threat threads'.

I screamed past the stupid monkey on my bike so fast that he barely had a chance to yell at me, much less throw anything nasty. I skidded to a stop right in front of the first threat thread and saw that it was still stretched across the path. I pushed the bike under it, stooped below it myself and then went on to check the other ones. None of the other threads had been tripped either, so I knew that the coast was clear. When I got to the mango tree, I leaned my bike against the trunk and climbed up.

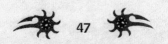

Billy and Todd got there ten minutes later.

'OK, the meeting is at order,' I said presidentially. 'Billy, you go first, then Todd and then me. What's the mission gonna be?'

Billy scratched his red crew cut and put a look of fake concentration on his face. It was fake because we already knew what each of us wanted to do for the weekly mission, but we always acted like we'd just thought of it.

'I say we build a huge jump on the banks of the river down below Ocelot Hill,' said Billy. 'We could start from the top of the hill and get up enough speed to jump across the river.'

Todd and I looked at each other with raised eyebrows. The river was about thirty metres wide and there was no way we'd be able to fly across it to the other side. Even if we did, we'd end up crashing when we landed.

'That's loco,' replied Todd. 'I say we sneak into Pablo Malo's banana field and steal some bananas.'

Todd always seemed to do what little thinking he did with his stomach. Some of his other ideas had been to sneak into the commissary at night to steal a case of orange Fanta, sneak into the Charles's house and put pairs of our underwear in

Denise and Cathy's dresser drawers and once he suggested that we sneak into Chris and Scott's trailers and put monkey poop in their beds. His ideas all had something to do with sneaking or food or both. I sure hoped that he wouldn't grow up to be a criminal and end up in jail.

'We'd never get past the dogs,' replied Billy, shaking his head. 'Even if we didn't get our legs chewed off by Loca, they'd raise a racket barking at us and Pablo Malo would come a-runnin'. I don't want to mess with him.'

'You believe everything you hear?' said Todd. 'I just think you're chicken.'

'My parents told me to stay away from him,' replied Billy. 'That's good enough for me.'

'Well, I don't think Todd's is such a bad idea,' I said. 'Our missions aren't supposed to be easy, but they are also not supposed to be impossible. Jumping the river's impossible, so I think Todd's idea is better than yours.'

Todd looked at Billy with a smug expression. It was my turn.

'I say we go to the airstrip and race the supply plane when it takes off at two o'clock,' I said. 'We'll hide in the bushes at the end of the strip.

When the Cessna turns around to take off, we'll sneak up behind it and race it.'

I thought it was a great idea. Billy and Todd didn't.

'We'll end up getting chopped to pieces by the propeller,' cried Billy. He was really worried because he knew that I was the President of the Machacas, and I had a little more sway than he and Todd had.

'Let's vote, and you can't vote for your own idea,' I said. 'All in favour of racing the Cessna?'

Todd and Billy didn't say anything. All I heard was the loud piercing noise of the cicadas in the jungle.

'All in favour of killing ourselves trying to jump over the river?'

Only the cicadas voted for that idea.

'Well, I guess we're going to go and steal some bananas.'

We hid behind a thicket of tall bamboo trees. Our bikes were behind us, leaning against the trunk of one of those huge spiky trees, ready for us to jump on when we made our escape. The

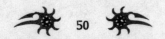

red dirt road that ran along the barbed wire fence that defined Pablo Malo's farm was just a metre in front of us. It was full of potholes with muddy red water in them from the big rainstorm the night before. If you went down the road to the left for about a mile you'd end up at the trailer camp where Billy and Todd lived. If you went to the right for a couple of miles you'd come to the washed-away bridge that used to go over the river. The rows of green banana trees started just on the other side of the barbed wire fence across the road. There were banana trees as far as you could see to the left and right. We knew that Pablo Malo's adobe farmhouse and storage barn were right smack in the middle of the orchards, and we knew that no one would be in the orchards working because it was Saturday. Since it was Todd's idea, he was the one who had to carry the machete that we'd use to cut down a banana stalk.

'OK, looks like the coast is clear,' I whispered. 'Now all we have to do is go to the nearest bunch of bananas that looks ripe, cut it down and get the heck out of Dodge. Got it?'

'Yep . . . ready.'

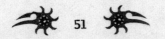

'Roger wilco.'

We were just about to step out from the cover of the jungle when we heard the sound of a truck engine coming from the right of us.

'Hold it,' I said, putting my fist up in the hand signal – universally known in military sneaking language – meaning *freeze*.

As the engine noise grew louder and the truck got closer, we crouched down lower and lower. The beat-up, army green jeep came around the bend, bouncing and splashing through the potholes. A cloud of bluish smoke poured out of a muffler that wasn't doing a good job of muffling anything. The canvas top had been taken off and we could easily see who was driving. It was Pablo Malo.

He had a battered straw hat on his head and his stringy black hair was flying around his neck in the wind. He wasn't wearing a shirt, which was pretty smart given how hot it was. A cigarette was stuck between his yellowish teeth and the smoke from it blended in with the burning-oil smoke of the old engine behind him. As he got closer I could make out the face I had only seen a couple of times before in my life. The whites of his eyes were bloodshot. Not exactly like the ones I'd see in some of the parents in Campo Mata when they'd had too much to drink, but more like when someone's been in the sun too much without wearing sunglasses. The hollow parts of his sunken cheeks were chock-full of pits and bumps, and so was his neck just under his sharp jaw. Seems he had had a bad case of acne when he was young. Guess that's what would happen to Chris Sanders's face when all his whiteheads finally oozed out and went away.

There were three dogs in the back seat of the jeep and one of them was Loca. She was a Dobermann-German shepherd mix with a bad temper and a lot of long sharp teeth. The other two dogs were mutts. I saw a couple of other things just before Pablo Malo passed by our hiding place and went on to wherever he was going. There were several cardboard boxes in the front passenger seat, and they were all wrapped up for shipping somewhere. I also saw a big white scar that stretched from one side of his neck to the other, right across his Adam's apple. It looked to me like someone had tried to slit his throat one day. The last thing I saw

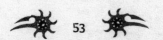

was the shotgun leaning against the cardboard boxes.

We all took a deep breath when the jeep rumbled past us. We didn't move until we could no longer hear the engine.

'Well, at least we don't have to worry about the dogs,' said Billy. 'I swear that Loca looked right into my eyes.'

'They didn't see us,' I replied confidently. 'Let's go and get some bananas.'

We ran across the dirt road, climbed over the fence and walked down a row of banana trees. The bunches of bananas in those trees were pretty green, so we kept on walking looking for some riper, yellower ones. We were in pretty deep when we decided that none of the bunches was going to be ripe enough to eat and we were about to give up the mission, when we saw the red Spanish-tiled roof of Pablo's farmhouse.

'I say we sneak up to the house and take a look,' whispered Todd. 'There might be some ripe ones in there.'

'I don't think that's such a good idea,' replied Billy. 'I mean . . . they say Pablo Malo is a really bad customer.'

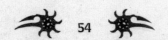

'And he has a shotgun,' I chimed in.

'Aww, come on, guys,' said Todd. 'We agreed to this mission, and the Machacas never give up on a mission.'

Well, that did it of course. We had no choice but to follow through on our mission to find some ripe bananas.

We reached the last bit of shade under the wide leaves of the trees. The adobe house was surrounded by a covered veranda that wrapped around the whole building. There were some hammocks strung out between some of the posts that held up the mossy tile roof of the veranda. Some scraggly plants grew out of the nooks and crannies of the roof. There were two arched windows to either side of the big wooden door that led inside the house. The door was closed and there was a large padlock on it. We could hear the sound of chickens coming from somewhere on the other side of the house, probably near the barn. Other than that – and the non-stop whining sound of the cicadas – we didn't hear or see anything.

'I'm gonna look inside,' said Todd, proving again that he wasn't the smartest kid on the block.

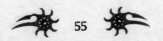

'I don't think that's such a good idea,' said Billy again. 'I think our mission should be aborted. We can try this one again, once the bananas turn yellow.'

But Todd was already slinking like a lizard towards the closest window, so Billy and I followed him and pretty soon we were all three standing with our backs to the cool adobe wall, side by side. I was the closest to the window, so I peeked through the windowpane and looked in.

I'm not sure what I expected to see, but whatever it was, it wasn't what I ended up seeing through that window. It was a big dining room with vaulted ceilings and whitewashed adobe walls, but that was about the only thing normal about it. There were stacks and stacks of wooden furniture piled to the ceiling, taking up most of the right side of the room: mahogany tables and chairs and dressers and bed frames. Each piece of furniture was wrapped in clear plastic, like they were ready to be picked up by someone.

There was a doorless hallway on the far side of the room that led to the bedrooms, or maybe to the kitchen. On the left side of the room there was a metal office desk with a fluorescent lamp, a

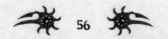

big flat paper map and a bunch of radio equipment on it. I couldn't tell what area the map covered, but I could see the squiggly lines that showed all of the high spots and low spots of the ground in that area. My dad had once showed me some maps like the one on the table. He said they used them to decide how they were going to get to some place in the jungle where they needed to set up a drilling rig.

The radio equipment was a mess of knobs and dials and wires everywhere, and there was a pad of paper and a pencil in front of the equipment. There was nothing on the walls and no other decorations around; not even a house plant or throw rug. Pablo Malo certainly wasn't using the room for dining. It was half storage room and half something to do with the map and the radio.

And then I saw them, next to the pad of paper in front of the radio equipment . . . a pair of silver spurs! It didn't take me long to jump to a conclusion. I turned around to my buddies and when they saw the expression on my face, their eyes got real big, real fast.

'Let's get out of here, and now! Don't ask any questions, just run.'

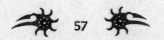

We started to run in the same direction we had come from . . . and straight at Pablo Malo!

There he was, just standing there looking at us with a cigarette burning between his teeth, his lips pulled back in a menacing smile. He had his shotgun in his right hand with the business end of it pointed casually at the ground. Standing next to him were Loca and the two mutts. Loca's lips were pulled back just like Pablo Malo's, only her teeth were a lot more pointed and sharp.

'Little *gringos*,' he said in heavily accented English. 'What you think you do? What you see?'

We didn't stay to talk. Just like we had trained ourselves to do, we took off, running away from him and straight into the cover of the banana trees. When we got into the shade we split up in three different directions. We heard Pablo laugh out loud.

'Loca . . . *ataque*,' he commanded.

I didn't look back, but I heard the snarls and barks of Loca and the mutts as they started out after us. I ran like the blazes. I could hear Billy screaming like a girl off to my right. Suddenly I heard the *boom* of the shotgun and a high-pitched

scream of pain coming from Todd off to my left. Pablo Malo had actually shot him!

I thought about going over to help, but I knew that there was nothing I could do but get shot myself, so I kept running. I crashed through the wide low-hanging banana leaves. I looked over my shoulder and saw what I was praying I wouldn't. Loca was gaining on me and she was going to sink her fangs into me any moment. I reached around to my back pocket and pulled out my slingshot. I knew I only had one chance. It had worked for Billy a couple of days before.

I stopped in my tracks, turned around to face the dog and pulled back on the thick rubber bands of my slingshot as if I were going to let loose a rock at her. Loca skidded to a stop about five metres in front of me, snarling and showing her rows of killer teeth. She was ready to pounce but she had learned respect for the weapon I had in my hand. The only problem was that I didn't have anything in the sling to shoot at her. I wanted to pick up a rock, but that would mean that I'd have to take my eyes off her and one of my hands off the slingshot. It was a stand-off. I backed up a step and Loca took a step forward. I didn't see any way she'd let me walk backward all the way home. I was in a real pickle and I was scared to death. The dog was going to kill me and eat me up. I was sure of it. My parents would never know what happened to me.

'I've got ya covered,' said a familiar voice behind me.

It was Billy and he had his slingshot aimed right at the dog. Loca was now looking from me to him, but she didn't look like she was ready to give up.

'Reach into my back pocket,' whispered Billy. 'I've got a bunch of marbles there and they're brassies.'

Without taking my eyes off the dog, I reached back and felt around his green jeans until I found his pocket with the brass marbles. I pulled out two of them and quickly loaded my sling with one. Now it was two against one.

'Here's the plan,' I said. 'We can't stay here much longer. Pablo's going to be looking for Loca and he has that shotgun. I'm going to let loose at Loca and try to bean her on the snout. I'll reload as quickly as I can while you keep ready to shoot her with yours if she decides to attack. OK?'

'Sounds like a plan,' came his reply from behind me.

I aimed that brassy right at the tip of Loca's nose and I pulled the rubber back further than I ever had before. Billy and I were dead aims with our slingshots and we could pick off flying birds if we wanted to, so I wasn't worried about hitting what I was aiming at. I was worried that it would only make Loca madder and that she'd attack us in a bloodthirsty rage. I let go of the rubber and the marble smacked into the dog's nose with a bone-cracking sound. Loca let out a pained yelp and took off towards the house, screaming and screeching in that horrible way that dogs do when they've really been hurt. It was the same sound that the Fultons' dog made when Mr Fulton accidentally ran over its leg backing out of the driveway. Billy and I didn't wait around. We took off towards our bikes.

When we got into the shaded safety of El Monte we doubled over with our hands on our knees trying to catch our breath. Todd's bike wasn't up against the spiky tree. That meant that he was still alive, or at least he was when he got on his bike. We jumped on our bikes and made a beeline

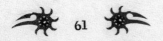

for the hideout. It didn't take us long. We didn't even care that we had torn through the threat threads getting there. We would fix them later. Todd's bike was on the ground at the base of the mango tree. We scurried up the wooden planks and into the tree house. Todd was sprawled out on the floor, moaning and groaning.

'He's gonna die!' cried Billy. 'Look at all the blood.'

There was blood all over the back of his legs. I went over and knelt beside him. He just kept moaning, like he was about to pass out from the pain. Billy was muttering 'Oh no' over and over again. I took my T-shirt off and wiped the blood from Todd's leg. With all of the blood wiped away it didn't look so bad. There were only three little holes in his leg and I could see something stuck in one of the holes. I pulled whatever it was out with my fingers and wiped off the blood. It looked like a small piece of clear sand. All of a sudden I figured it out.

'It's rock salt,' I cried out. 'Pablo shot Todd with rock salt! He's not going to die. He'll just need some medicine and Band-Aids. I better get the other pieces out so it'll stop stinging so much.'

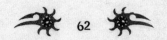

Billy stopped his chanting and even helped me pull out one of the salt pebbles. Todd squirmed a little, but he didn't complain. We pulled up Todd's shirt and saw where the rock salt had hit him there too, but those hadn't gotten through his shirt and broken the skin. He was going to have some black and blue marks, but they'd go away soon enough. Todd was going to be fine.

'That better?' I said to Todd.

'Yeah,' he replied weakly. 'Thanks.'

'So what did you see that made you want to hightail it outta there?' asked Billy.

'Remember when we saw the body of the dead guy?' I replied. 'Remember his fancy belt buckle and silver tipped boots? You notice how his boots were rubbed and worn where the spurs normally go?'

'Yeah . . . so?'

'Well, I saw a pair of silver spurs on the table in Pablo Malo's house and those spurs match the silver boot tips and the belt. They were given to the dead guy after he won some rodeo some- where, or maybe he got them as a gift – I don't know. But I am sure that they were all part of the same set.'

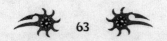

'Are you thinking what I'm thinking?' replied a wide-eyed Billy.

'Yep . . . either Pablo Malo killed him, or he knows who did.'

Chapter 5

Bombitas

The day after the scare at Pablo Malo's farm, everything seemed fine. Todd didn't tell his parents the truth about the holes in his leg and all the polka-dot bruises on his butt. He told them that he'd fallen off his bike on a gravel road. I was pretty sure they didn't believe him, but I was also sure that they didn't think that he'd been shot by a madman with a shotgun either. I had to bury my bloody T-shirt, and I told Mom that I'd left it next to the river when we'd gone swimming and that I would go back and get it when I could. She probably didn't believe me, but she didn't make a big deal out of it.

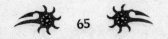

I could hear my parents running around the house getting ready for the Fourth of July party that they were going to have that evening. Just about everybody in Campo Mata would be there. Billy had slept over at my place. He was still asleep in the bottom bunk, snoring, and it was starting to bug me. I was trying to finish reading *The Hobbit* and I only had a few pages to go, but Billy's snoring was driving me crazy. I slammed the book shut hoping that would wake him up, but it didn't, so I jumped down from the bunk and walked out of the room heading for the bathroom down the hall. When I got there I grabbed the plastic cup we always kept by the sink to rinse out toothpaste and filled it up with cold water. Then I went back to my room and stood over Billy. His mouth was wide open, so when he was about to inhale another noisy gulp of air, I poured the whole cup of water down his gullet. That woke him up. He sat straight up, coughing and hacking, madder than a Tasmanian devil.

'Avery McShane . . . I oughta kick your butt,' he spluttered. 'Dang it.'

He took a swing at me, missed and almost fell out of the bed in trying.

'Wakey, wakey,' I said cheerfully. 'It's Independence Day! It's party time!'

Fourth of July was everybody's favourite holiday around the camp, not just for the adults, but the kids too. Billy's mad face turned into a smiling one when he realised what day it was.

'Oh yeah,' he said, rubbing the cobwebs out of his eyes. 'We gotta go buy some firecrackers.'

'Well, you might as well go and pretend to take a shower and brush your teeth,' I replied. 'When you're done we'll go to the safe and get some money.'

Billy got up and headed for the bathroom while I made his bed. I always had to promise Mom that I'd tidy up the room before she would let me invite someone over to spend the night. I don't think Billy even knew how to make a bed.

Billy came back with his same old clothes on, except for his boots, which were by the front door. Mom didn't let anybody come into the house with shoes on. Of course Billy's hair wasn't even the least bit wet.

'Dad told me that Capitán Gómez wouldn't let the fireworks truck into camp this year,' I

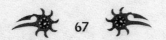

said. 'Guess he wasn't too happy about last year when those boxes of firecrackers blew up and nearly burned down the commissary. So now everybody has to go to the airstrip to buy fireworks.'

'I still think that Chris and Scott were the ones who lit up that box of firecrackers,' replied Billy. 'They were there when it happened, and I saw them pointing at it and laughing about it.'

'Yeah, for sure it was them,' I said. 'You know, after we buy the fireworks, I think we should drop by and talk to Capitán Gómez about Pablo Malo and the spurs and all.'

'Maybe we can collect the reward,' said Billy.

'You want to tell our parents what we've been up to?' I said. 'I don't think that's such a great idea. Besides, we don't actually know who did it.'

'I guess you're right,' replied Billy. 'My dad would ground me for a month if he knew that we'd been there trying to steal bananas, but we can't just sit on the information, I suppose. What about your dad? Can we trust him? He's always cool about these sorta things.'

'My dad's cool, but not *that* cool. I'd get in

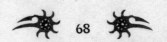

68

trouble too and I don't want to get grounded either. I think we can trust Capitán Gómez. I mean, he seems like a nice guy, and I don't think he'd tell our parents if we ask him not to.'

'Sounds like a plan, but we need to get him to promise not to tell before we let him in on this, OK?'

'I'm with you.'

'We'd better get going,' replied Billy. 'We've gotta buy the best fireworks before they're sold out.'

We turned our bikes on to the short dirt road leading into the pipe yard and after a few pedals crossed over the cattle guard and made our way down the middle of hundreds of stacked drill pipes. Mati didn't like crossing cattle guards so he went around it and under the barbed wire fence. Billy and I had both taken off the playing cards that we usually left on the front forks to make our bikes sound like motorbikes. We were going to get our money from our hidden safe and we didn't want to attract any attention. Since it was a holiday there weren't any eighteen-wheelers around loading pipe, and no one was in sight. When we got to the aluminium workshed on the far side of the yard, we leaned our bikes up against it and walked around to the back of the building. That's where our safe was. All of the money that we'd earned finding golf balls was in it.

Manuel Ortega, who was the supervisor of the pipe yard, had helped us make the safe. He spent about an hour cutting and welding together some pieces of scrap steel. It ended up looking like a metal shoebox with a hinged door on top and a latch for the combination lock we bought at the commissary. Then he welded it on to a big, super-heavy manhole cover, so it would take a crane to steal it. We figured if someone went to that much trouble, they could have it.

We cleared all of the tumbleweeds off the canvas tarp that camouflaged the safe and then pulled off the tarp. I got on my knees and grabbed the combination lock in my left hand and began to twirl the combination knob.

'Eight . . . thirty-two . . . twelve,' I said as I worked the lock.

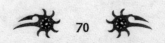

'Avery, you don't need to say it out loud,' whispered Billy. 'You never know if someone's listening.'

'Do you see anybody here?' I replied as the lock clicked open.

Mati was busy scratching off some fleas that must have been camping behind his ears, but he stopped when he heard the click. I reached in and pulled out a wad of bolivars wrapped together with a rubber band.

'How many bolivars should we take?' I asked.

'I don't know . . . maybe a hundred and fifty?' replied Billy.

'That's almost all we have,' I said.

'Yeah,' said Billy, 'but this is for a good cause.'

'I'm with you,' I said.

I pocketed the whole wad, closed the top of the safe and locked it. Billy pulled the tarp back over and we scattered branches and dirt over it again. We looked around to see if anybody had seen us, but we knew that no one was around because Mati hadn't barked.

We took the shortcut through El Monte to get to the airstrip. It saved us about twenty minutes compared to getting there on the asphalt roads

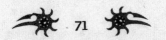

through Campo Mata. We came out of the jungle at the far end of the airstrip, near the place that I had planned to have us wait for the Cessna to turn around to race it. I was still a little sore with Billy and Todd for not choosing my mission instead of almost getting killed at Pablo Malo's place, but at least I knew that they'd probably go for my mission idea next Saturday.

We saw the red flatbed Chevy parked by the yellow one-storey building on the left side and halfway down the runway. The building was where Guillermo Santos, the customs agent, would check all the stuff that the Cessna brought into and took out of Campo Mata. There were only three rooms in there. The main one had a big table with a two-way radio on it, a few sets of rubber stamps, an ink-pad and one in-and-out box full of all the customs paperwork. Guillermo, who was really fat and smelly, never seemed to get up from his chair behind the big desk. Most of us figured that he just slept in the chair. There was a stinky bath-room with a toilet that didn't work most of the time. The third room was where all of the stuff that came in and out on the Cessna was stored.

That door was always closed and locked and we'd never seen inside. Guillermo kept the keys to both of those rooms on a key chain clamped to one of his belt loops.

Billy and I raced down the middle of the airstrip. We'd put the playing cards back on the forks of our bikes and the noise as they clacked in the spokes got louder and louder the faster we went. Mamba beat Billy's rust bucket, as usual. It never was much of a contest. We jumped off our bikes next to the flatbed full of fireworks. A thin old man sat on one of the hundreds of cardboard boxes that were stacked on the ground in front of the truck. He looked like he was about eighty years old, but it was hard to tell. He stood up and smiled at us, showing us the last five or six teeth he still had in his mouth. At least they were really white.

'*Chicos*, you are the first ones here,' he said in Spanish.

Well, that was good news. We didn't really know when he'd show up, so we were worried that the best stuff might already be gone.

'Two boxes of sparklers, four boxes of string firecrackers and thirty rockets,' I replied. 'Oh

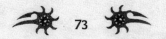

yeah, if you have anything new this year we'd like to see it.'

The old man looked us both over like he was trying to decide if he could trust us. Then he stood up and walked over to the cab of his big truck. He motioned with his arm for us to come over there, so we did. He opened the car door and pointed at two boxes in the passenger seat of the cab.

'*Chicos*, these are *bombitas*,' whispered the old man as he looked over our shoulders at the window of the airport building. Seems he was making sure that Guillermo wasn't watching us, but we knew that the fat man couldn't see us from the chair that he never seemed to leave. 'They are illegal to sell, but I can sell some to you young men if you promise not to tell anyone where you got them. Can I trust you?'

'Absolutely,' said Billy.

'Cross my heart and hope to die,' I replied almost at the same time.

'OK then. They cost a lot more than the other fireworks,' whispered the old man. 'That is because they are very powerful. Each one is really half of a stick of *dinamita*. You must make

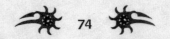

sure to keep them in a cool place until you use them. They have longer fuses than normal fire-crackers so that you can be far enough away to not blow yourselves up. I will give you another roll of fuse line so that you can tie on some more if you want.'

Now *this* was cool. Billy had a big smile on his face, even though I knew he was trying to act all adult-like and responsible. We both knew that we shouldn't buy them, but that wasn't going to stop us. This was going to be great.

'We'll take eight of 'em,' I said.

The old man ended up getting all of the bolivars that we'd taken from the safe. We were a little short of money for everything we'd wanted, so we had to give up some of the usual strings of fire-crackers and sizzlers. But we didn't give up the *bombitas*.

The fireworks were in plastic bags hanging from our handlebars and we were just getting on to our bikes to head back to camp when we heard the sound of the Cessna's single engine in the distance. That meant that it was just about ten

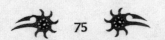

o'clock in the morning. We looked out in the direction of Caracas, to the north, where the plane always took off from and always went back to. It was just a speck in the light blue sky.

Then we heard the sound of a different type of engine coming down the dirt road leading to the customs building. We recognised that one too. It was the sound of Pablo Malo's jeep. Billy and I looked quickly at each other, jumped on our bikes and made a beeline for the first path into the surrounding jungle. When we got into the cover of El Monte, we hid our bikes – being sure to take off the playing cards – and sneaked our way back to the edge of the trees.

We could see the front of the customs building and in the distance the jeep bouncing down the dirt road, covered in a cloud of blue smoke. A minute later the beat-up jeep lurched to a stop in front of the building and Pablo jumped out. He looked the same as he had the day he and Loca attacked us, but this time he had left the dogs at the banana farm. Guess he wasn't taking any chances on us again. The jeep was only about twenty metres away from us. I could see the shotgun propped up in the passenger seat next to a couple of taped-up shoeboxes. We could hear the sound of voices coming from inside the building, but we couldn't tell what they were saying.

'I'm gonna try to get closer and spy on them,' I whispered to Billy. 'I want to know what they're saying.'

'You're nuts,' hissed Billy. 'No way, don't do it.'

'They're up to something and I want to know what it is,' I replied. 'You go on back to camp and take my bag with you. I won't want to be lugging that thing around if I have to hightail it outta here. I'll meet you back at my house. Make sure you hide the fireworks under my bed.'

'Avery, please don't do it,' pleaded Billy. 'Pablo will kill you if he catches you.'

'Don't worry about me. I can take care of myself. You go on. I'll see you in a bit.'

Billy sneaked his way back to the bikes, grabbed my bag of fireworks and left me there alone. I was about to come out of the shade of the trees when the front door to the building swung open and Pablo came out. He walked over to the side of the jeep closest to me, picked

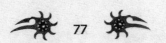

up the shoeboxes and then went back inside, this time without closing the front door. I could hear the sound of the Cessna's engines getting louder. I stepped out of El Monte and ran on my tiptoes to the nearest wall of the customs building. I was pressed up against the wall like a leech on a leg. I skirted along the wall until I was right next to the open door and listened to them talking.

'This is the last time, Pablo,' said Guillermo. 'It is getting too risky. Capitán Gómez has been nosing around here a lot more lately.'

'I will tell you when enough is enough,' growled Pablo Malo. 'I pay you more than you're worth and you are already in this way over your head. And don't worry about that police chief. I will be taking care of him soon. You just stamp the boxes and put them on the plane.'

'But I can't keep doing this. Someone will find out sooner or later, and when they do I'll be thrown in jail. They will toss the keys in the river.'

'That's not going to happen. With Gómez out of the way, we'll never have to worry about getting caught,' replied Pablo. 'The plane is

almost here. I've got to use the bathroom. Give me the key.'

I heard the rattle of keys, followed a moment later by the opening and closing of the bathroom door. I knew that Guillermo's back was to the front door because he always faced the airstrip. I peeked around the doorway and saw the fat man's back as he dabbed a rubber stamp on the ink-pad and stamped one of the boxes. I made certain that Pablo was in the bathroom. When I pulled my head back I saw the shotgun in the passenger seat of the jeep. That gave me a great idea.

I didn't stay at the airstrip much longer. When I heard Pablo Malo come out of the bathroom, I skedaddled out of there and went straight to the golf club to find Capitán Gómez. I saw the police car in the parking lot of the club when I got there. It was there almost every Saturday. Gómez loved to play golf with the *gringos* on his days off, even though he was terrible at it. He had even played a few rounds with my dad when I caddied for him. They both liked to drink beer when they played, although my dad never drank

when it was a tournament. By the time they reached the last hole they were always in great moods and talking really loud and laughing all the time. Orange Fanta never made me act like that.

I walked into the clubhouse, past the golf shop and the locker room and out of the back door, where all the caddies stood around waiting for the golfers to pick them.

'*Hola*, Avery,' said Raul, who was my favourite caddy.

'*Hola*, Raul,' I said. 'Have you seen Capitán Gómez?'

'Yeah, he teed off about an hour ago,' he replied. 'He's probably on seven or maybe eight.'

'Thanks,' I said. 'I'll try to catch him at the pond. *Hasta luego.*'

I got to the eighth tee just ahead of Gómez. His playing partner was Mr Slater, who would normally be playing with my dad except that my dad was helping my mom get ready for the party that night. Both men smiled and waved when they saw me and I did the same back.

'*Hola*, Avery,' yelled Gómez.

'Hi, Capitán. Hi, Mr Slater,' I said.

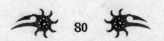

I didn't expect to see Mr Slater with the police chief and I was wondering if this was going to be the right time to talk to him.

'Umm . . . can I talk to you, Capitán?' I said. 'It'll just take a minute.'

Mr Slater raised his eyebrows, but then he started to walk over to the tee to take his shot over Mata Pond.

'I'll just go on ahead,' he said. 'We'll hook up at the clubhouse.'

'OK,' said Capitán Gómez. 'I'll be right behind you.'

The police chief turned back to me.

'So what brings you all the way out here to talk to me?' he said with a pleasant smile.

'I need to talk to you about Pablo Malo.'

The smile vanished from his face. He looked down at me with a really concerned expression. His forehead grew a bunch of frown marks that I hadn't seen before and the sparkle in his eyes disappeared just like that. Now I was really, really wondering if it was such a good time to talk about Pablo Malo. He put his hand on my shoulder and made me walk with him away from Mr Slater and out of hearing distance. He kept

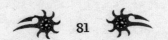

his back to the tee and made me stand in front of him.

'You must stay away from that man,' he said. 'He is very dangerous.'

'I know,' I replied. 'Billy and Todd and I found that out the hard way.' I waited a second then made up my mind to follow through and tell him what I knew. 'Remember the day you brought in the dead guy who had been shot?'

He nodded.

'Well, before you chased us away, I noticed that he was wearing a fancy belt buckle with matching silver tips on his boots.'

'Go on,' he said.

'The buckle and the tips were part of a set. I've seen lots of gauchos who've won rodeos wear them. They always come with a matching pair of spurs. The dead guy was missing his, but I saw the wear marks from them on his boots.'

'I'm listening,' said Capitán Gómez.

I told him all about what happened during our mission to steal bananas. He listened very carefully and he did not interrupt me even once. His hands were on his hips the whole time.

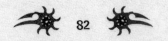

'So that's what happened then,' I said. 'But there's more that's happened today.'

I filled him in on Guillermo Santos and what had been said in the customs building. When I was done he pushed his golf cap back on his head and scratched his forehead. He pulled the cap back down and looked at me. He smiled and then sort of chuckled, shaking his head from side to side at the same time.

'Well, that is quite a story, young man,' he said. His pencil-thin moustache smiled at me. 'You are like a curious cat, aren't you?' Then he grew more serious. 'But this is a dangerous situation. You cannot go back into El Monte to your hideout until I have investigated further. Do you understand me? Pablo Malo is a bad man. I have known this for a long time. It is said that he has killed men down in the diamond district, but no one has been able to prove anything. I will make a visit to the banana farm on Monday.'

'Capitán, I will stay out of El Monte if you promise not to tell my parents about all of this,' I replied.

That made him laugh again.

'I can promise you this. I will not tell your

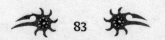

parents unless it is absolutely necessary. That is the best I can do. OK?'

I could tell that was the best offer I was going to get from him.

'OK,' I said.

Chapter 6 🌞

Next Time No Salt

The orange sun was about twenty minutes from disappearing below the horizon. People were starting to show up at our house for the Fourth of July party. There were cars parked all along the street and now some folks were parking their cars on the street behind our house, close to the fence that kept out El Monte.

All of the doors to our house were open. My dad had set up tiki torches in the field behind our house. I counted twenty-four of them, and next to each one was a wooden picnic table with an American flag tablecloth on it. My mom and dad were standing next to our big outdoor barbecue

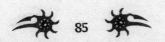

pit talking to the Slaters and the Fultons. The pit was closed but clouds of hickory smoke poured out from the edges of the heavy steel cover. There were two other huge barbecue pits on flatbed trailers parked next to ours and smoke was coming out of them too. I'm guessing that they must have had about three whole cows and who knows how many pigs cooking. My dad and some of his golfing buddies always drove over to Anaco – which was the nearest real town – about a week before the party to pick out the animals that we were going to eat.

Someone inside the house changed the music from rock and roll to Brazilian samba, which is what happened whenever the adults wanted to start dancing. I grew up listening to Latin music, and the first song was one of my favourites – it put me in an even better mood. And it wasn't just me. In the windows I could see the silhouettes of adults who had started dancing to the cool beat.

Billy and Todd came out of the back door and walked over to where I was sitting in one of those fold-up aluminium picnic chairs. They had brought their own chairs, so when they got to me they set them up and sat down too.

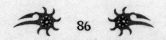

'Billy told me what happened at the airstrip,' said Todd. 'Sounds like Pablo and Guillermo are up to no good.'

'Yeah, but I haven't figured out what just yet,' I replied after taking a swig of my 7Up. 'I think Capitán Gómez has an idea, but he wouldn't tell me.'

'You think we can trust him?' said Billy. 'Gómez, I mean.'

'Sure. He's a cop,' I replied. 'If you can't trust a cop, who can you trust?'

'Yeah, I guess so,' said Billy, 'but I'm more worried about him telling our parents about us trying to steal bananas.'

Billy's parents were really strict, and he'd get into even more trouble than Todd and me if they found out we were trying to steal things – even if it was just bananas.

'Don't worry about it,' I said. 'The secret's safe with him.'

'Hey, guys, look at that!'

Todd was pointing up in the sky to the left of us. It was a dark cloud of something and it was moving towards us, getting bigger. Some of the adults had seen it too. Then I saw Mr Slater

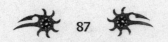

looking at something right above where we were sitting. My eyes followed his just in time to see a huge flock of birds flying right over us, heading straight for the approaching black cloud. It took a second for everyone to remember what was going on, because it only happened a couple of times a year.

'The swallows and the queen machacas,' I yelled out. 'They're back! This is so cool.'

The clouds of bugs and birds were going to collide pretty close to us. It looked like the swallows were going to have a party that night too. And then it happened. All of a sudden there were swallows diving down and flashing around, snatching up all of the flying queen ants they could eat. The yellow light from the tiki torches reflected off the birds as they zipped around like bats. After a while you could even smell that strong, nasty odour that squashed ants gave off when you stepped on them.

There must have been a million of those flying ants in that black cloud, but they were taking heavy casualties and losing the battle with the birds. Little pieces of ants, and some whole ants, started to rain down on the ground around us. I

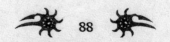

picked up one of them, careful to keep my fingers away from the humongous pincers. Billy and Todd did the same thing. Holding the huge queen ant in the fingers of my right hand I aimed its pincers at the tip of the thumbnail of my left hand. They were opening and closing, trying to get a piece of me. When the pincers felt it, they chomped down and the two sharp ends buried themselves in the tip of my fingernail. Once those pincers got buried the queen ant couldn't – or maybe just wouldn't – open them. They were stuck on for good. Like we always did, I pinched the ant's body off. All that was left on the tip of my fingernail was the ant's head. The three of us did this ten times; once for each fingernail.

'You guys ready?' I said. 'Let's go and creep out some girls.'

Even though we did it every time the birds and ants had their awesome battle, the girls always obliged us by screaming and running away. And we always obliged them by running after them, yelling at the top of our lungs with our machaca fingers reaching out to get them.

Denise was right in front of me running as fast as she could and looking back in freckle-faced

horror at my ant-zombie fingers. She was taller than me, and I think that she could run faster than me but she wasn't. Maybe fear slows you down. Her blonde ponytail was flopping around on her shoulders and her yellow sundress kept swishing this way and that. I guess that she'd finally had enough when she all of a sudden stopped in her tracks and turned around to face me. Not expecting it, I almost ran smack into her. Somehow I managed to dodge her but in doing so I tripped and fell on the grass and almost knocked over one of the tiki torches. She stood there looking down at me with a mad look on her face and her hands on her hips. I could hear Billy chasing Denise's twin sister, Cathy, somewhere near the barbecue pits. Todd had probably given up early to grab something to eat.

'Avery McShane,' she said, 'when are you going to grow up?'

I got up and swatted away the big clod of grassy dirt from my knee.

'I figure when I reach five feet,' I replied. 'At least that's the plan.'

'Well, I'm already five feet and I'm too grown-up for this nonsense.'

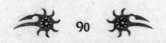

She looked mad, but I knew she wasn't. Denise was my girlfriend. I knew it, and everybody else in Campo Mata knew it. She seemed to be the only one who didn't know it. At least she didn't act much like she knew it.

'Yeah, well, you might be taller, but I'm still older than you,' I replied. 'By almost three months. So who's more grown-up?'

'You are so immature,' she hissed back. 'You'll still be a kid when you're forty, if you live that long.'

She stuck her tongue out at me, then ran away in the direction of her sister's screams. I hoped that Billy would give up the chase before Denise got there. Two mad Charles twins against one skinny Billy didn't seem like good odds. Still, all in all, I was happy to have had a nice chat with my girlfriend.

The party had been going on for hours. It was nearly midnight, and that's when all the fireworks were set off. The adults were laughing and talking at each other in really loud voices like my mom would talk to my grandma who was hard of

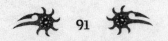

hearing. The fireworks show was set up on top of the Campo Mata Circle. Our house was one of ten that lined the outside of a road that was a perfect circle. There was a big grass field in the middle on the other side of the road from the houses. It was mowed once a week by one of those tractor mowers. A long cement sidewalk led straight up the middle of the field and ended up at the steps in front of a raised concrete structure that the pilots could see when they flew over the camp. It was about twenty metres across and looked like a huge cement coin lying flat on the ground, except instead of the head of some famous president there was a big red star painted on it. The star was the symbol of the oil company that my dad worked for. The Circle is where all the biggest celebrations took place, and it was perfect for the fireworks show. By now everybody was standing in the field around the Circle.

Since many of the people who worked for the oil company were engineers, they spent a lot of time and money to make sure that the fireworks show was fantastic and that it'd go off without a hitch. The engineers had it all planned out. They would only have to light one fuse and the

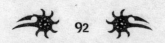

92

fireworks would start shooting up, one at a time, for almost ten minutes. Since my dad was the Chief Engineer – and since we were the hosts of the party – he got to light the fuse. Someone had already turned off the music, so when my dad flicked on his lighter, the crowd hushed and everything got real quiet. My dad bent down and lit the fuse and the sparkly flame started working its way across the floor of the Circle to the piles of waiting fireworks. It got closer and closer and then it all began.

The fireworks were great. Some would go way, way up in the sky before exploding in a round shower of red, or white, or blue. Our eyes always saw the explosions before our ears heard them. It went on and on, and I hoped it would never end. In between each burst it would get dark and you couldn't see anyone, even the person next to you. The fireworks were so bright that they made it hard to adjust your eyes when they weren't going off. When they exploded you could see the bright, smiling faces of all of the people looking up, most of them with their mouths wide open. In one flash I saw Billy standing on the other side of the Circle next to his parents, in another I saw the Charles

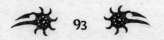

twins hugging each other and looking up. And then in another flash I saw him. He was just standing there, right behind Todd. He was looking straight at me. It was Pablo Malo.

When the next set of fireworks lit up everything, he was gone. I wondered if I had just imagined it. I had taken a few sips of a Cuba Libre that my dad forgot about earlier, so it could be that I had gotten a little drunk. I tried to convince myself that it was just my imagination, but I wasn't fooling myself. It was him all right and he wanted me to see him. If he was trying to scare me, it was working.

The party was over and everybody was gone. Folks would be coming by tomorrow to help clean up, but most of them had some sleeping-in to do first. I was in the bathroom getting into my PJs. When I'd thrown my clothes in the laundry hamper, I moved over to the sink to brush my teeth. I looked at myself in the mirror. Normally, after a party like that, I'd have a smile on my face and be all ready to get a good night's sleep. But I was pretty sure that I wasn't going to sleep too well that night. I brushed my teeth and turned off the bathroom light. I walked down the hall and into my parents' room. They hadn't gotten ready for bed yet. They each gave me a hug and told me to 'sleep tight' and to 'not let the bedbugs bite'.

I walked into my bedroom and pulled back the sheets before going over to the switch on the wall to turn off the lights. And there, taped over the light switch, was a piece of white paper with a note scrawled on it. My eyes opened wide in shock when I read it.

Next time no salt.

Chapter 7

War

I slept with my parents the night of the Fourth of July party. Pablo Malo had been in my house and even in my room. He knew where I lived and he probably knew who the rest of the Machacas were. So there was no way on God's green earth I was sleeping alone.

I woke up way after my parents did, which was not the way it normally happened. I was a morning person, so I was usually up before them. But it had taken me a long time to fall asleep, thinking about Pablo Malo waiting to kill me, so I slept in. The sun was already pretty high up in the sky. I could tell because the sunrays were coming almost

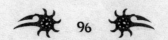

straight down through the window, instead of shooting across the room like they do when the sun's just coming up. The smell of scrambled eggs and bacon wafted into the bedroom, and I could hear my parents talking in the breakfast room next to the kitchen.

'Lolita's going to sub for Nelly this week,' I heard my mom say. 'I told her to take all the time off she needs.'

'Fine with me,' replied my dad. 'I still don't think we should tell Avery about all this yet.'

I wondered what it was that they wouldn't tell me, but I knew better than to try to wrangle it out of them. They'd tell me when they were good and ready. I got out of bed and walked down the hall picking the sleepy bugs from the corners of my eyes.

'Hi, Mom. Hi, Dad,' I said, just before yawning with my mouth open.

'Morning, Avery,' they said at the same time.

'Cover your mouth when you yawn,' added Mom.

'Sorry,' I said.

My mom went into the kitchen to get me some grub and I sat down in the chair next to my dad.

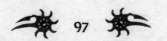

He looked pretty tired from last night, but he seemed to be in a good mood anyway.

'Helluva show last night, huh?' he said with a satisfied grin. He hadn't shaved and since it was Sunday, I didn't expect he would until tomorrow morning before he went to work. He had on a pair of Bermuda shorts and a polo shirt, so I guessed he was leaving soon to play golf.

'Yeah, real cool,' I replied.

I guess I wasn't too convincing.

'What kind of answer was that?' he said. 'Sounds like you didn't like it much.'

'Oh, it was awesome all right. I guess I haven't woken up yet.'

'Hmm, OK,' he said. 'Well, I'm off to conquer the greens. See ya later.'

He put his knife and fork together on his plate and took the plate into the kitchen.

'See you later, honey,' he said to Mom just before I heard the smack of their goodbye kiss.

The screen door to the carport slammed shut and I heard the truck start up. The tyres crunched on the gravel in the driveway and then stopped when he reached the asphalt road. I listened to the growl of the car engine fade away

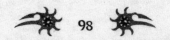

in the distance. Mom came in with a plate full of eggs and bacon, which she put down in front of me before she went on down the hall to her bedroom.

'I'll be at the Smiths' all afternoon playing bridge,' she yelled out from the bedroom. 'If you go somewhere, be sure to leave a note to let us know where you are, and don't forget to lock the front door.'

Of course I left the house, and I even left Mom a note. I told her I was going to the swimming pool at the club instead of where I was really headed. I was going to check on the hideout. Even though Capitán Gómez had made me promise not to go into El Monte, I couldn't stand the thought that something might have happened to it. The situation had changed when Pablo Malo showed up at the party and invaded my house, so I figured Gómez would understand. If Pablo Malo knew where the Machacas lived, he might know where our hideout was. Besides, I had Mati with me and I was going to ride my bike in case I needed to make a run for it.

Stupid Monkey only managed a couple of quick squawks before we were out of his range. Mati didn't even bark at him once. Seems he knew that we were on a dangerous mission and needed to move as silently as possible.

The first threat thread was still there, so we passed under it and I walked my bike in the direction of the next one. It was still there. I could see the top of the mango tree from where I was, but I couldn't see the tree house. We Machacas always checked each one of the threat threads before we showed ourselves to anybody who might have invaded the hideout. We fancied ourselves as sneaky as Apaches when we checked on the threads, and with all that was going on, I was being careful not to make any noise. Mati wasn't making any either.

The next two threads were still strung up, but the fifth one had been tripped. The black thread was hanging down from the branch on one side of the path. It was the same path that we'd taken when we went on our mission to steal the bananas, the path to Pablo Malo's place. This was not good news. My heart started beating fast and I began to sweat like a stuck pig. I leaned my bike against

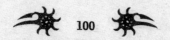

one of those spiky trees and knelt down next to Mati.

'Someone's been here, Mati,' I whispered in his ear. 'They might still be around. You need to be super quiet, like a doggy ghost, OK?'

Mati smiled at me with his tongue hanging out and cocked his head to the side. He knew what I was talking about. I didn't bother to check the last threat thread. I started to work my way in the direction of the hideout. Mostly I crawled on my stomach, sometimes on my hands and knees. I only stood up when I could hide from view behind the thick trunk of a tree.

It took me almost half an hour to get in sight of the tree house and by then I was dripping in sweat and itching like the dickens from rubbing up against different bushes and breaking through some cities of spiderwebs. Worse, I was still smarting from a machaca soldier ant that bit me on my ankle when I tried to shimmy my way over one of their highways on the ground. His head was now stuck on one of my fingernails, so he'd paid the price. There was no movement from the tree house and the only thing I heard was the cry of a bird or two every now and then,

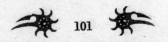

and of course the non-stop whine of the cicadas. If someone was in there, they probably wouldn't have been able to hear me sneaking up over the high-pitched sound of those big bugs. Of course, I wouldn't have been able to hear them either.

Mati hadn't barked yet, so I was pretty sure no one was around. He would know and he would start barking, even though I'd made him promise not to. He was a dog after all. I waited for another couple of minutes and then stood up and took a step out of the jungle cover and into the open. I was standing on the outside of our ditch, trying to look tough and ready, but inside my soul I knew the only thing I was ready for was to start running the other way. Nothing happened, so I took another step forward. And still nothing.

'I'm coming in, so if you're in there, this is your chance to give up,' I called out.

There was no answer, and Mati still hadn't barked. I was pretty sure now that I was alone, so I walked bravely to the trunk of the mango tree without taking my eyes off the open window of the hideout. I put my hand on the first wooden plank leading up through the hole in the floor of the tree house. Everything looked all right from there. I started climbing up and when I got to just below the opening I held my breath, then poked my head up through it and looked around.

It looked like a tornado had landed inside. The stacks of comic books had been torn apart. Almost every page of each one of them was ripped in two. There were broken jars all over the place and the bugs and worms and fish that we had kept in them were scattered on the floor. The floor was still wet with alcohol in some places, so whoever had done this hadn't been gone for long. It smelled like a hospital. The shoeboxes with our butterfly and moth collections were stomped flat. Someone had taken a knife to our holsters and cut the leather belts in half and left them on top of the pile. Even the barrels of our six guns had been bent almost in two.

At first I felt like crying, but instead of doing that I just got mad. I knew my face was red already and getting redder. I stood up inside and started pushing stuff around with my sneakers. The only things that I knew for sure were missing were the *Mad* magazines that Todd had stolen from his parents' room. They were some of our most prized possessions, so I was getting fiercely angrier with each passing minute.

'Goll dang it,' I yelled. I started kicking torn comics and boxes all over the place like a Viking gone berserk. 'This just chaps my red butt.'

I stopped when I heard Mati bark from somewhere below. I sneaked over to the window and saw Mati looking out in the direction of the path to Pablo Malo's place. I went from madder than a one-legged ant to girly-scared in one second. Was that him? If it was, I knew I was toast. I wasn't much for praying, but I was doing a lot of it right about then. Mati barked again and then he started to let loose with a long, mean growl. Now I was thinking how they'd be finding my dead body with pee and poop in my underwear.

'Mati, it's just me,' I heard from behind the bushes. 'Good boy.'

It was Billy and I had never in my life been so glad to see him. He came out from his hiding place and Mati ran up to him. Billy got on his knees and did the usual hugging and petting that everyone does to a smiling dog. He looked up and saw me in the window.

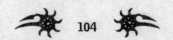

'I saw that someone had tripped a threat thread, so I was sneakin' up,' he said. 'When I saw Mati I figured everything was clear. You all right? You look like you've seen a ghost.'

'Get your butt up here. You're not gonna like what you see.'

It took us a long while to clean up the mess. We stacked the ripped-up comics as best we could. We'd be bringing a bunch of rolls of Scotch tape to put them back together. We pushed the shoeboxes back into shape and put the butterflies and moths that hadn't been smushed to a pulp in them. I cut my finger on a piece of broken glass when we were picking them up, but it didn't bleed for very long.

We said a cowboy eulogy for our six guns, like they did in the westerns, and then buried them in the dirt under the mango tree. We dug another hole for the bugs that had been in the jars and put them in there along with all of the broken glass. The last thing we did was let the big worm go free since his jar had been busted to pieces and we didn't have another one to use.

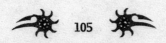

'Pablo Malo just bought into the game,' said Billy in a soft West Texas gunslinger's drawl.

'He sure did,' I replied as I stamped down the last clod of dirt over the bug grave. 'This means war.'

Chapter 8

The Jungle at Night

Billy got permission from his parents to sleep over
again at my house the night after the party and
then to sleep over at Todd's house the next night.
Todd got the OK from his mom to sleep at my
house too, but he told them that he'd be staying
at the Hales' the next. I told my dad that I'd be at
Billy's and then at Todd's. We pretty much didn't
have to ask. We usually told our parents where
we'd be staying and they'd just let us be. During
the summer break we were always sleeping over
at each other's houses. What they didn't know
was that we wouldn't be sleeping at any of our
homes for the next two nights. We were going to

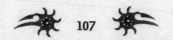

be at the hideout the whole time. We were getting ready for the war with Pablo Malo. But I had some things I needed to do before we all got together at the tree house later that evening.

Mati was running next to my bike as I whooshed down the main street of Campo Mata. I was headed to the police station to talk to Capitán Gómez and let him know what had happened at the party and at the hideout the day before. It was about two o'clock in the afternoon, and it was as hot as the dickens out. I figured that Gómez would be back from lunch and back from his visit to Pablo Malo's farm. He had told me that he was going there first thing Monday morning. I couldn't wait to hear about that and I couldn't wait to throw some fuel on the fire with my news about Pablo invading my house and trashing our hideout. I rounded the curve by the school like a motorbike racer with my left knee almost touching the ground and the playing cards in the forks clacking really fast and loud. The police building was right ahead, but I could already see that Gómez's car wasn't in the parking lot in front of it, so I was hugely disappointed.

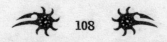

'Dang it!' I yelled over the noise my bike was making.

I skidded to a stop in front of the parking place reserved for Capitán Gómez. There was a sign in front of it that read, *Policía Nacional – Reservado*.

'You stay here, Mati,' I said. 'I'll be right back.'

I leaned Mamba against the wall, walked up the steps to the front door and knocked.

'*Adelante,*' I heard from inside, so I opened the door and went into the cool, air-conditioned building.

Lieutenant Sánchez was sitting behind the reception desk, shuffling through a stack of official-looking papers. He looked up and smiled when I came in, and put his pencil and papers down.

'Señor McShane Junior,' he said. 'To what do I owe this great pleasure?'

Lieutenant Sánchez was a young Venezuelan, and this was his first job after graduating from the police academy in Caracas. He had showed up about six months earlier, full of energy and ready to catch all the bad guys. Problem for him was that there never was much crime in Campo Mata, so I was pretty sure he was bored all the time. He was well built and liked to wear tight, short-sleeved uniforms that showed off his

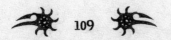

muscles, and the young Venezuelan women were always flirting with him.

'I came to see Capitán Gómez,' I said in a casual way, like I was always coming to talk to him about criminals and crimes. 'I guess he's not in 'cos I don't see his police car.'

'I have not seen him since last Friday,' replied Sánchez. 'I do not know where he is. I tried to raise him on his radio a couple of times this morning but I have not been able to.'

Well, that was bad news. My mind started racing when I heard that, but I tried to look calm.

'Maybe his batteries died,' I suggested.

'It could be,' he replied as he leaned back in his chair and clasped his hands behind his head. 'But it is not like him. He is always here early, getting the paperwork done before going out on patrol, and he always tells me where he's going.'

I didn't know the Lieutenant well, so I didn't know if I could trust him. He was a policeman – and I usually trusted all of them – but something told me to hold my tongue about what I was thinking might have happened, so I did.

'Well, if he shows up, could you tell him I dropped by?'

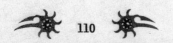

'Sure thing, *amigo*,' he said.

Holy smokes, I thought. Had Pablo Malo killed the Capitán? I had overheard Pablo Malo telling Guillermo that day at the airstrip that he would 'be taking care of him soon', but I didn't think he meant that he'd kill him. If he'd kill a police chief, he'd for sure kill a *gringo* and maybe even a *gringo* kid like me. This whole thing was getting down-right scary. Mati and I took off for home.

I was in my bedroom packing up all the stuff I thought we'd need to carry out the war. I had already jammed my backpack with the *bombitas*. We didn't have any of the smaller firecrackers and stuff left over because we had set them off at the party, but we had kept the big ones to set off later in El Monte when no one else was around. I had thrown in my toothbrush and a change of underwear because I knew my parents would check to see that I had. I didn't want them going over to Todd's or Billy's to bring them to me. If they did, our whole plan would fall apart and we'd end up being grounded for the rest of our lives. Each of us had a list of things

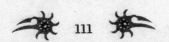

that we needed to bring to the hideout and I was double-checking mine.

Pocket knife
Sleeping capsules
Flashlight (plus extra batteries)
Bombitas *(and fuses)*
Walkie-talkies (plus extra batteries)
Lighter
Slingshot (plus extra ball bearings)
Black T-shirt
Dog leash
Dog food
Cub Scout canteen (with water)
Ten candy bars
Can of bug spray
Camera

I had all of the stuff, except for the *bombitas*, laid out on top of my bed. I put the knife and the sleeping capsules that I had taken from my mom's medicine cabinet in my front jeans pockets. I stuffed the rest into the backpack as best I could and lifted it up to test the weight. Even though it was really heavy, I decided that I would probably

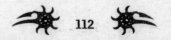

be able to make it to the hideout without breaking my back. I jammed the flashlight into the left back pocket of my jeans. The other pocket was loaded with small ball bearings and my slingshot.

I was just about ready to leave. The sun was glowing orange through my window, so I knew that I only had about half an hour to reach the hideout before it got dark. I didn't want to be alone on the path in the jungle when darkness fell, Mati or no Mati.

'I'm gonna hit the road now, Mom!' I yelled. 'Remember I'll be at Billy's tonight and Todd's tomorrow, so don't worry about anything, OK?'

'Wait . . . hold your horses,' she yelled back from down the hall somewhere.

She was going to check my backpack to make sure I had everything I needed for two nights away. She'd see the *bombitas*!

'I packed my toothbrush and two pairs of under-wear,' I said. 'Gotta go . . . it's getting late.'

'OK, sweetie,' she said. 'Don't forget to actually use that toothbrush.'

'Roger that,' I replied. 'See ya.'

That was a close shave, I thought.

I put my arms through the straps of the bulging

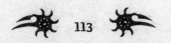

backpack and hoisted it on to my back, then slung the strap of the canteen over my shoulder. Just before turning out the lights, I remembered to grab my Dodgers baseball cap and put it on. I trudged down the hallway, through the kitchen and then out of the screen door to the carport. Dad's car wasn't there because he'd gone to play darts with his buddies at the club.

'Come on, Mati,' I whispered as I got on Mamba. 'It's time to go to war.'

The inside of our hideout was lit up by the bright white light of the Coleman lantern that Todd had borrowed from his dad. We were all sitting cross-legged on the wooden floor facing each other. All of the stuff that we'd brought from home was scattered in front of us.

'You didn't forget the machetes, did you?' I asked Todd.

'I left them leaning against the tree trunk,' he replied.

'You got the rope?' I said.

'Yep,' he replied.

'OK, good. Looks like we didn't forget anything,'

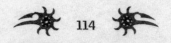

I said in my best President-of-the-Machacas voice. 'Let's go over the plan one more time.'

As usual we argued about different parts of the plan, but we finally came to an understanding. Billy always got uptight about the dangerous parts of any plans or missions that we thought up, but we all knew that when the chips were down he'd do his part. Todd was usually too dumb to realise when things were going south, so he never seemed to panic.

'I'm still thinking that maybe we should tell our parents what's going on,' said Billy. 'Maybe they'd understand and take care of this mess without us getting killed.'

'Billy, we've already been through this,' I said. 'We'd end up getting grounded for trying to steal things and for lying all the time. It's too late anyway. They think we're sleeping over at each other's houses, and if they find out we're not, we won't be able to see each other ever again. So just drop it, OK? Besides, we're the ones that started this and we're the ones that need to finish it,' I went on. 'Now Capitán Gómez has probably been killed and it's our fault. This is our war and no one else's.'

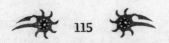

'Avery's right,' said Todd. 'We got ourselves into this mess and anyway, if my parents find out about all this, they'll probably send me to boarding school in the States. They told me they'd do it if I kept getting into trouble, and this would probably do the trick.'

'Oh all right,' said Billy, shaking his head. 'But I don't like it. Pablo Malo's probably already carved a notch on the butt of his shotgun for Gómez. If we're not super careful, he'll be carving three more on it.'

Chapter 9

Out of the Fire . . .

We stood on the ground underneath the mango tree. It was nine thirty at night. Each of us had on black T-shirts and we had smudged mud all over our faces and the backs of our hands. We were now in maximum sneaking mode. I was finishing tying the muzzle on Mati's snout, which he never cared for, but we couldn't risk him barking at the wrong time and he was being a good sport about it. The Coleman lantern was turned down to the lowest level up in the tree house and just a few rays of yellow light came peeking out of the places where the boards weren't fitted together so well and out of the open window. We had our packs on

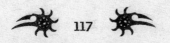

our backs, full of our weapons and gear for the war. Todd's was by far the heaviest because he was bigger and stronger than Billy and me.

'Machetes and slingshots?'

'Check,' all three of us said at the same time.

'Flashlights, pocket knives and binoculars?'

'Check.'

'Lighters?'

'Check.'

'OK, then. We're all ready to go.'

I picked up Mati's leash and led the way in the direction of the path to Pablo Malo's farm. Billy was right behind me and Todd brought up the rear. He wasn't nearly as freaked out about walking around in the dark as Billy was.

'Did you tell my parents that I loved them?' asked Billy.

We had left a note in the tree house for our parents in case we didn't make it back from the mission because Pablo Malo had killed us.

'I already told you I did,' I replied without turning around. 'And I wrote down everything we know about the silver spurs and Pablo Malo and Capitán Gómez, so stop worrying about it, OK?'

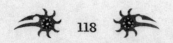

I knew Billy well enough to know that he'd keep on worrying, but at least he stopped fussing.

It took us a long time to sneak up on Pablo Malo's adobe house, especially the last hundred metres or so. If Loca caught wind of us and started barking and carrying on, we'd be in serious trouble. But we'd been lucky so far. The moon was just a thin sliver low in the night sky and it wasn't casting much light. There were lots of stars, and we had no problem picking out the planets. Venus was the one with the bluish light and Mars was the one with the reddish light. Of course, the easiest constellation to see was always Orion's Belt, and it was hanging right over us.

We were all three lying on our stomachs two rows of banana trees back from the lawn in front of the house. Our backpacks were on the ground next to us. Yellow light poured out from the two windows on either side of the front door. The two mutt dogs were curled up on the covered porch in the light under the window to the right. There was no sign of Loca, which made the hair on the back of my neck prickle. I tapped Todd on his shoulder.

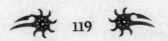

'Hand me one of the meat balls,' I whispered.

He reached into the top of his pack and pulled out the big wad of wax paper that we'd wrapped around the ground meat. There were six balls of raw ground beef and each one had a bunch of sleeping capsule powder in the middle of them. Todd handed me one.

'Here goes,' I whispered. I launched the meat ball like I'd seen G.I. Joe lob grenades in the comic books, and it landed with a soft thud on the grass in front of the porch. The mutts didn't move a muscle, and neither did we. I could hear Mati behind us, sniffing in the smell of the raw meat.

Todd handed me another meat ball and I tossed that one too. It landed a little closer to the mutts and this time their heads popped up at the same moment. They looked around and we could see their noses sniffing for danger. One of them got up and started following his nose to the left and right, tracking down the source of noise. The other one got up too and started to do the same thing. They moved towards the meat grenades side by side until they came to the first one and one of the mutts just gulped it down without a second thought. The second mutt – feeling gypped,

I guess – nipped at the snout of the other mutt and then started sniffing around to beat his buddy to the next one, which he did, swallowing the grenade in one quick chomp.

'Put the meat away,' I whispered to Todd. 'They might follow the smell all the way here.'

I didn't think they would though, because we had made sure to sneak up downwind of the house. It had all been part of the plan. We had tons of experience sneaking up on unsuspecting animals from when we went out on one of our hunting missions in El Monte, and had learned a long time ago about upwind and downwind. You had to be pretty good at it to get close enough to hunt with slingshots.

The mutt dogs gave up trying to find more of the meat grenades after about a minute and went back to where they had started and curled up again as if nothing had happened. We didn't know how long it would take for the sleeping drugs to take effect, but I knew that my mom would take one of those capsules and sleep like a rock for the entire night and we had emptied three whole capsules in each of our meat grenades. Since those mutts weighed a whole lot less than

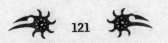

121

my mom – not that she was very big, because she wasn't – we figured it wouldn't take too long for them to go nighty-night.

I checked my watch. It was ten thirty-three. We waited for about fifteen minutes before I pulled out my slingshot and loaded it with a ball bearing. I looked for something to shoot at that would make a loud enough noise to wake the mutts without being loud enough to hear from inside the house. I saw a big red clay pot with a rubber plant growing in it over to the right of the house on the edge of the gravel drive that led around the back to the big barn. I aimed at it, pulled back the thick rubber band and let loose. The ball bearing hit the clay pot right in the middle with a louder-than-I-had-hoped-for crack. The pot shattered, the dirt inside it came pouring out and pretty soon after that, the whole rubber plant fell over with a pretty-easy-to-hear-from-the-inside-of-the-house rustle of leaves. I held my breath, Billy and Todd held their breath, and Mati stopped sniffing. Heavens to mergatroid, I thought. That had ended up being a heckuva lot louder than I had planned.

'You dingbat!' hissed Billy. 'Why not just shoot at the window?'

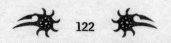

122

I couldn't argue with him about that.

All of our attention was on the front of the house. The mutts on the porch didn't look up or even twitch, so I figured they were out for the count. That was the good news. The bad news was that we heard the sound of voices coming from inside the house. Suddenly we saw the dark silhouette of a man appear at the window right above where the mutts were curled up and unconscious. I could tell that it wasn't Pablo Malo, and for sure it wasn't that fat man Guillermo either. This guy's outline was way taller than either one of those two and he was super muscular, like G.I. Joe. It took me a moment or two to realise who it was, but it was Billy who said it out loud.

'That's Lieutenant Sánchez,' whispered Billy. 'What's he doing here?'

We could see him bring his hands up to the sides of his face and lean up against the window, looking around. He looked down at the sleeping dogs and I guess he figured that there wasn't much going on outside if the dogs hadn't gotten up to bark and make a fuss. He turned away from the window.

'*No es nada*,' I barely heard him say.

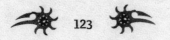

Whew, that was too close for comfort, I thought. Billy was still fuming at me.

'That was a dumb fool thing to do, McShane,' he said. 'Even Todd wouldn't have done that. No offence, Todd.'

'None taken,' replied Todd.

'Well, nothing happened and we're still on schedule,' I said defensively. 'Let's go around the back and peek in on them.'

We stayed in the cover of the banana trees that surrounded the house and the barn. We still didn't know where Loca was, so we took a long time making sure not to step on any dry leaves or branches that might give us away. Now we were upwind of the house. By the time we made it to the back of the house it was almost eleven o'clock. The barn was over to our left about fifty metres away and we could see a faint light peeping under the bottom of the huge doors at the front.

Since Billy was the scarediest of the Machacas, he was the best at sneaking. We sent him in to check out the goings-on in the house first, before we moved on to the barn. He crawled on his stomach like a World War One soldier slinking from one bunker to the next. When he got to the wall of the farmhouse he stood up and shimmied along it until he reached the only window on that side of the house. We saw him peeking in and we could tell from the way he cocked his head that he was listening to some sort of conversation going on inside. After about five minutes he worked his way back to our hiding place in the orchard.

'Well, what's up?' I asked him when he got back from his reconnaissance mission.

'It's Lieutenant Sánchez all right,' he said. 'Pablo Malo and Guillermo Santos are in there with him. They're drinking beers in the kitchen, and from the look of it they've been drinking a lot. There are empty bottles all over the place.'

'What're they talking about?' asked Todd.

'I'm not really sure,' replied Billy. 'Pablo Malo said something about how next week's shipment would be the biggest one so far, and Guillermo was saying that they couldn't keep this up much longer before they'd get caught. Sánchez laughed at him and told him to shut up and do his job. He was acting like the boss of them.'

'A shipment of what?' asked Todd.

'I don't know, they didn't say, but I can bet it's really illegal and worth killing us for.'

'They say anything else?' I asked.

'Yeah,' replied Billy. 'Pablo Malo said that he'd dump the body in the river in the morning.'

The dead guy on the concrete slab had already been buried, and we hadn't been shot and killed yet, so we guessed that they meant that they would be dumping Capitán Gómez's body into the river. It was around this time that I started to wish that I hadn't forced Billy and Todd to go on this mission. Billy was right. We should have gone to our parents with the problem and let them work it out. It still wasn't too late for that, and I made up my mind that we'd give up the mission and head home. If we ended up being grounded for the rest of our lives, at least we'd be alive and not floating face down in the river.

'OK, change of plan,' I said. 'I think we'd better go back home and tell my dad about all of this. He'll know what to do.'

I figured that Billy would be the first to agree to that idea, but he totally surprised me by what he said next.

'I think we owe it to Capitán Gómez to find his body and keep these guys from throwing it into the river for the caymans to eat,' he said. 'I'm

pretty sure they wouldn't keep a dead body in the farmhouse, so it's either in one of the cars over there or in the barn. I'm guessing the barn.'

Todd surprised me too.

'Billy's right,' he said. 'It's the least we can do. Those guys are getting so drunk that they'll be passing out in a bit, so it should give us a fightin' chance. Between the three of us we should be able to drag the body to the hideout at least.'

Right about then I was real proud to be a Machaca.

'OK then,' I said. 'Let's check the barn first. Don't forget about Loca – she could be anywhere.'

'I saw her lying on the floor in the kitchen with the bad guys,' said Billy.

'Whew,' I said.

The most obvious way to get into the barn was right through the front doors, but we didn't want to chance that because those big doors could be seen from the kitchen window of the farmhouse. With the light inside the barn, the bad guys in the house might see us if we went in through those doors. We sneaked around to the back of the barn looking for another way in. We were now totally hidden from view from the farmhouse, so I turned

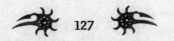

on my flashlight and pointed it at the wall of the barn, searching for another entrance. Barns in Venezuela are built with cinder blocks and bricks and concrete so we weren't just going to pry off a few planks of wood with our machetes to get inside. In fact, the building that we were looking at wasn't really so much a barn as a place to store the equipment used on a farm, such as tractors and carts that were loaded with bananas during the harvest.

The beam of my flashlight moved around on the wall until it fell on a small window above us. There was a little bit of light coming from it, but we hadn't been looking up and didn't notice it until now.

'That's the only way in,' I said.

'I don't see a ladder,' replied Todd. 'It's too high to reach.'

'Not if I climb up on your back,' I said.

So I climbed up on Todd's back. He got on his hands and knees next to the wall and I put my right sneaker on his shoulder and stood up, then I brought up my other foot and put it on his other shoulder. Then, with a whole lot of strain and moaning, Todd stood up to his full height. My

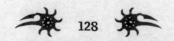

hand reached the sill and then I felt the pane of glass. I pushed on it and it opened up to the inside.

'I think this'll work,' I said. 'I'm going to have to push off pretty hard though, so get ready.'

'Ready,' grunted Todd.

I bent my knees a bit and then jumped up as far as I could. I managed to get my elbows on the ledge just far enough to lever myself up and in. I was on the rafters and I could see down to the ground floor, only there weren't any tractors or farm implements in there. Instead there was a big flatbed truck with a stack of long logs on it and against the wall there were several industrial-size saws and other kinds of woodworking machines I didn't recognise. There was sawdust all over the floor. A bunch of half finished pieces of wooden furniture was stacked up in a jumble on the other side of the truck. One lonely light bulb hung down on a wire right over the cab of the truck. I stuck my head back out and looked down at my buddies. Todd was brushing the dirt off his shoulders.

'Toss up my backpack,' I whispered.

Todd threw it up and I snatched it out of the air.

'It looks like a furniture factory in there, which

129

would explain the stacks of the stuff in the dining room in Pablo Malo's house,' I said, keeping my voice low. 'I haven't seen anything else out of the ordinary yet.'

'Seems weird to have a furniture-making business in the middle of a banana farm,' said Todd, scratching his head.

'Maybe Pablo Malo makes a little money on the side in the off season,' suggested Billy.

'Could be,' I said, 'but I smell a rat. I'm going in to look for the body. If I see it, I'll jump down to the ground floor. I won't be able to come back out of this window if I do that, so the only way out will be through the front. You guys go around to the corner of the building and hide in the shadows near the barn doors. Keep an eye on the kitchen window of the farmhouse and listen out for me.'

'Roger that,' said Billy.

I turned back and carefully looked around the inside of the barn.

The logs in the truck bed looked like they came from mahogany trees, which meant that they came from the deep jungle. Almost all of those kinds of hardwoods had already been cut down in the area around Campo Mata, so I figured Malo

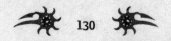

had them brought in from pretty far away. It wasn't illegal to harvest mahogany trees if you had a permit from the government. I was beginning to think that maybe I had been wrong about the silver spurs and that all of this had been a big misunderstanding.

And then I saw the body.

🔆 Chapter 10 🔆

. . . Into the Frying Pan

The body was in the shadows in the far corner of the barn, close to the doors. All I could really make out from where I was were two knee-high black boots sticking out of the shadows, lit up by the lonely light bulb. The rest of the body was hidden behind a stack of wooden crates. I looked around for a way down that wouldn't mean having to leap from the rafters. I figured I probably wouldn't break my leg if I had to make the jump from that far up, but I was sure that it'd be painful. I decided my best bet was to work my way across the rafters, beam by beam, until I got to where the crates that hid the body were stacked up, so that's what I did. It was a cinch to get down from there.

Once I made it to the ground floor, I walked around the crates over to where the black boots stuck out. My heart was beating hard, like it had when I started to pull the bloodstained sheet off the dead guy on the concrete slab. I pulled out my flashlight, turned it on and pointed it at the spot where I expected to see the rest of the body.

It was Capitán Gómez all right. He was in a sitting position with his back up against one of the wooden poles that held up the cross-beams above it. There was blood all over the front of his khaki shirt and his head was slumped down on his chest, so I couldn't see his face. His arms were behind him, so I figured that they were still tied up from when they killed him. I bent down on one knee beside the body, without taking the flashlight beam off him. My hand was shaking as I reached out to the body. I took a deep breath, lifted his head up by his chin and shone the flashlight beam on his face. He had been brutally beaten and his eyes were closed. His lips were split in several places and I saw that his cheekbone showed through a really bad

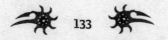

gash. There was a big swollen bump on his forehead where I guessed that someone had kicked him with a heavy boot. I was just about to move the flashlight when I saw his chest moving a little on its own. He was taking a breath. He was still alive!

I put my backpack on the ground and reached in and pulled out my canteen. I opened the top and gently pushed his head back until I could pour some water into his torn-up mouth. When the water hit his mouth, he began to cough and spit and then he opened his swollen eyelids. Only one of them opened all the way, but when he caught a gander at me, that eye opened up really wide.

'Avery . . . what are you doing here?' he croaked. 'You must go . . . now. It . . . it is dangerous. They will kill you.'

'Shhh, Capitán,' I whispered. 'I'm not going anywhere without you.'

I got out my pocket knife and pulled open the blade. I moved behind Gómez and started to cut away at the rope that tied his hands. Since I always kept it sharpened I got through the hemp rope in a jiffy. Capitán Gómez groaned as he pulled his

arms away from the pole and placed his hands in his lap. He rubbed at his raw wrists. It was clear to me that he had tried hard to twist his hands out of the rope binding but had only managed to rub off most of the skin under it.

'Do you think that you can get up?' I asked.

'I can maybe manage that, Avery,' he sighed, 'but I cannot walk very far on my own. They have broken some of my ribs, and I am sure that I have a severe concussion from what those scum did to my head.'

'Why did they do this to you?' I said.

'They are smuggling diamonds in the logs,' he said as he tried to get up. 'They drill holes in the logs and stuff the diamonds in the holes. They use this furniture business as a front.'

I looked around again. Sure enough, I could see where someone had drilled a small hole in one of the logs that had been laid out on a long table with a saw at the end of it. You wouldn't notice the hole unless you were looking for it. Even if you did, you'd think that it might have been made by some boring beetle. It was a darn clever set-up. I turned back to the wounded police chief.

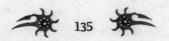

'OK, try to get up,' I said as I put his arm over my shoulder. 'Here, I'll help you.'

Using the pole and my shoulders Gómez managed to get to his feet, wincing and groaning all the way. He leaned against the pole, breathing hard. I could tell for sure that there was no way he could get very far without a lot of help. He needed a doctor.

'Listen, Capitán,' I whispered, 'it isn't just Pablo Malo and Guillermo who're in on this. Lieutenant Sánchez is part of the gang too. He might even be the leader.'

'Sánchez?' he said, looking me straight in the eyes. I could tell he didn't want to believe it. A corrupt policeman was the worst kind of scum to someone like Gómez. 'Are you sure? I cannot believe it.' He closed his eyes.

'He's in the farmhouse with the other two,' I said. 'Billy says he acts like the boss.'

'It was Pablo Malo that did this to me,' groaned Gómez. 'I had no idea about Sánchez.'

'Well, he's in it up to his neck,' I said, looking around. 'One thing I know is we've gotta get you out of here. Seems they think they've already killed you, and sure as shootin' they'll

finish the job if they find out you're alive. Pablo Malo said that he was going to dump your body into the river in the morning. Billy and Todd are waiting outside. Try to lean on me and I'll help you.'

I put my right arm around the man's waist and he put his arm on my shoulder for support.

'Just take it easy and lean on me as much as you need to.'

We shuffled our way slowly to the far side of the barn doors, near where I expected Billy and Todd to be waiting.

'Psst, are you guys there?' I hissed through the crack in the door jamb.

'Yeah, we're here,' replied Billy in a sharp whisper. 'Did you find the body? What's up?'

'Listen up. I don't have time to explain,' I replied. 'Keep an eye on the farmhouse. When you think I can open the barn door without being seen, let me know.'

I could tell that the Capitán was going in and out of consciousness because his eyes would close and his head would loll to the side every now and then, and when that happened it took all my strength to keep him on his feet. My muscles

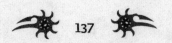

were really getting tired when I finally heard Billy's voice.

'The coast is clear.'

I pushed open the barn door only wide enough for us to fit through and then closed it behind us as fast as I could.

'Todd, I need your help,' I whispered.

Todd and Billy stood there open-mouthed for a long moment staring at Capitán Gómez before Todd moved over to take my place and helped to move Gómez into the cover of the banana trees.

'Holy guacamole,' whispered Billy. 'He's alive!'

'Let's get a little further away into the trees,' I said. 'We can talk about everything there. Come on, Mati, here, boy!'

Once we got about a hundred metres away from the barn, we set the police chief on the ground leaning against a banana tree. He hadn't eaten in a long time, so we gave him a couple of candy bars and some more water from my canteen. While Gómez rested I told Billy and Todd about everything that had happened inside the barn and about the diamond smuggling operation.

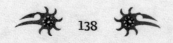

138

'Well, that explains why they'd want the Capitán out of the way,' said Todd. 'But it doesn't explain why they'd kill the gaucho.'

'Who knows,' I replied. 'But that doesn't matter right now. What do you guys think we should do? Capitán Gómez can't get very far, even with our help.'

Billy was drawing circles and lines in the dirt with his finger. He told us what his idea was without looking up from his doodling.

'We've got us a mite of a problem with Sánchez. He's got a badge and he's got them pistols,' he said, turning his voice into West Texas gunslinger mode, which he always did once he got to feeling brave and tough. 'And those boys might be checking in on the barn at any minute. When they find out that Gómez isn't there they'll come looking for us. We've left shoe prints all over the place and I bet they can read the signs of us *gringos*. First place they'll go is the hideout.'

'Yeah, Pablo Malo will let Loca loose and follow her to us,' I said. 'Lieutenant Sánchez will get into his police car and try to cut us off at the dirt road. It'll take us for ever to get there the shape

Gómez is in. We need to do something they wouldn't think we'd do.'

Todd was scratching at his crew cut and had a look of deep concentration on his face. It wasn't an expression we were used to seeing from him, so we waited for him to put his thoughts into words.

'We should split up like we always do, in three different directions,' he said. 'Since I'm the biggest I'll go with Gómez and help him along. One of you two will have to go and get help from some adults back at the camp. I think it should be Billy 'cos he's the sneakiest of us. Besides, Pablo Malo already knows where your house is, Avery, and maybe he doesn't know where Billy's is.'

We sat there for a minute thinking about it. Billy was probably already getting back into scaredy-cat mode thinking about wandering around in El Monte in the dark. I was trying to think of a place to take Capitán Gómez that the crooks wouldn't think of, and Todd was probably through thinking for the rest of the night.

Mati lifted his snout into the air and started sniffing around. The cicadas didn't make their whining noise at night, so the only thing we heard

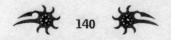

was the soft rustle of big banana leaves when a little breeze pushed at them. I gazed at the night sky. Orion's Belt was gone and so were the stars and planets. Clouds had moved in all of a sudden and I realised that Mati was feeling a change in the weather. It looked like we'd be getting soaked pretty soon.

'Whatever we do, we'd better get doing it,' I said, pointing to the sky. 'It's going to rain cats and dogs.'

Billy and Todd looked up when I said that.

'Oh, great,' whined Billy. 'Now I've gotta sneak around in the dark *and* in the rain. That just figures.'

Just then we heard a screen door squeak open and then slam back shut. Someone had just left the farmhouse and we all knew it would only be a matter of seconds before someone found out that Capitán Gómez had escaped. I had to think fast. We still hadn't agreed on a plan and I knew we had to get out of there. It took me a few seconds.

'OK, guys, here's my plan.'

*

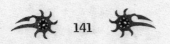

I was alone now. The other guys were carrying out their parts of the plan, and I was working my way back to the barn, using the banana trees for cover when, suddenly, the farm compound went nuts. Lights went on all over the place and Loca was barking like there was no tomorrow. I could hear Pablo Malo and the Lieutenant yelling at each other in Spanish.

'I told you those *gringo* kids were going to be a problem!' yelled Pablo Malo. 'You should have let me take care of them.'

'Shut the hell up, Pablo!' Sánchez yelled back. 'You cannot just kill little *Americanos* and hope to get away with it.'

'Well, it is what we must do now, eh?' replied Pablo. 'If you won't do it, I will. After we catch them I will deal with them, then let their bodies float downriver. If somebody finds them, they will think that they drowned in the flood. And the river *will* be flooding soon. It is going to be a big storm.'

'Whatever you do, I do not want to hear about it,' replied Sánchez. 'When we catch those *niños* I will turn them over to you. What you do with them is your problem.'

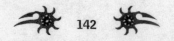

'That is fine with me,' replied Pablo. 'Loca, let's go find them.'

I wasn't wondering what would happen to us any more. Pablo Malo had made it perfectly clear, even though we'd sort of figured it out already. But a funny thing had happened. Instead of panicking, we had put our heads together and thought up the best plan we could to keep them from nabbing us. My fingers were crossed for my friends, for Capitán Gómez and for me.

Instead of sending Todd and the wounded police chief to the hideout, where they would for sure get caught, we decided that they should go in the opposite direction to the old water pumping station by the washed-away bridge. They were already on their way. We didn't think that the gang would guess that we'd be brave enough to actually go away from the safety of Campo Mata. They would figure that we'd head for the closest mom or dad to get help. In fact, Billy was on his way to get help and headed in the direction of the trailer camp, but he wasn't going to move along the dirt road or use any of the paths that we usually used to get around in El Monte. We had him take Mati to keep him from dying of a heart attack in the dark. As for me, I was crawling on my stomach, headed straight for the farm.

As if things weren't bad enough, the wind suddenly picked up like crazy and a big flash of lightning went off somewhere too close for comfort. I started counting under my breath.

'One thousand and one, one thousand and two, one –'

Blam! I nearly jumped out of my skin. That storm was almost on top of me. I was worried about Billy out there all alone, even though Mati was with him. Not only was he afraid of being by himself in the dark, but he had had a big problem with lightning ever since the day it had struck his trailer and fried all of the electrical stuff inside. I felt the first big drop of rain land right on the back of my neck, and then it really started to pour. I knew it was going to be a gully-washer. Most rainstorms in El Monte were like that. The moat around our hideout would be filling up in no time, and Pablo Malo was right about the river. It was going to flood, just like it did when it took out the bridge a couple of years back. I wasn't too worried about Todd and Capitán Gómez in the old pump house because it was high enough up on the bank of the river to stay dry. I was plenty worried about me.

The good news was that the rainstorm had probably already wiped out our footprints and it was going to be nigh on impossible for Loca to follow a scent. After all, she wasn't a bloodhound or anything, just four legs holding up a mouth full of fangs. I heard a car engine rev to life and the sound of tyres peeling out on the gravel. I was pretty sure that it was Lieutenant Sánchez tearing off to the red dirt road to cut off our escape back to Campo Mata.

I kept on sneaking towards the farm compound. By now I was more swimming than crawling since the water had started to pool in the ruts between the rows of banana trees. I could see the farmhouse and the barn, but I saw no sign of Pablo Malo or of Loca. I figured Guillermo, fat guy that he was, had stayed in the house to hold the fort while the other two went looking for us. He wouldn't be much use traipsing about in El Monte. It worried me greatly that I couldn't see Pablo and his killer dog, but I was determined to carry out my part of the mission. When I had told them what I was going to do, just before we split up in three directions, Billy had looked at me with his eyes as big as saucers.

'That's just plain loco,' he had said. 'You're going from the fire right back into the frying pan!'

Chapter 11

Seventh of July Party

It was the first time I was actually glad to hear Loca barking. I was happy about it because it came to me from pretty far away, in the direction of the path leading to our hideout. That meant that the only bad guy left at the farmhouse was Guillermo, and I knew I could run away from him if I needed to, so instead of practically swimming all the way to the barn, I got up and started walking. I kept in the cover of the banana trees but I wasn't much worried about being seen now that it was raining so hard you could barely see your hands in front of your face. It was still dark and it was going to stay that way for another couple of hours.

The door to the barn was partly open, which was a good thing. It meant that I could slip in pretty easily. The problem was that the light was still pouring out from the inside, which meant that I might be seen when I tried. I was snuggled up against the wall of the barn in the dark shadows under the eaves and out of the rain. I was soaked through and the mud on my face and hands was streaming down all over me. I must have looked like some sort of ghoul or zombie. I could barely make out the kitchen window of the farmhouse across the lawn, and I didn't see the outline of anyone looking out of it, so I took my chance and sprinted into the barn. I was sorely tempted to close the barn door, but I knew that it would probably be noticed by the fat man at some point, so I left it open and started working on the first part of my plan.

I leaned my machete against one of the wooden crates, took the pack off my back and set it on top of the same crate. I rummaged around in it and pulled out my camera. The outside of the case was a little wet, but the camera was dry. I put the strap around my neck and walked over to the log

148

that I'd seen the little hole in, on the long table. I stuck my finger into the hole and felt the end of a piece of cloth, but I couldn't pull it out. I looked over at the workbench to find a tool that might help and saw a pair of long tweezers hanging on a hook. It was probably what they'd used. I reached the long pincers into the hole and pulled out a small sack of oily cloth. I untied the string at the top and turned it over. Five clear pebble-sized rocks fell out on to the table. I knew what they were of course. My dad and his buddies had shown me ones just like these that they had found when they went panning for them on the banks of the Orinoco River on one of their annual trips. Diamonds!

I put the camera to my eye and started taking photos of the diamonds, the little sacks they came in, the hole in the log and some more of the rest of the barn. I thought about it for a second, before pocketing several of the diamonds. I decided it wasn't really stealing if I gave them to the Capitán after this was all over. He'd want the evidence.

Before I put the camera away, I pulled out the plastic bag with the *bombitas* and the roll of extra

fuse. I looked around for good places to put the mini pieces of dynamite. On the other side of the barn I saw one of those metal gas tins, the kind you usually see latched down to the back of some African explorer's Land Rover, only I was pretty sure this one was used by Pablo Malo on his jeep. I picked it up and shook it to see if it had any gasoline in it and could tell from the sloshing around that it was almost half full. I took the cap off and walked around the barn pouring gasoline on things that I thought would burn, especially on the logs in the bed of the truck and the wooden crates that I had used to get down from the rafters earlier.

I pulled out four of the *bombitas* and held them in one hand while I twisted their fuses together to make one big fuse. I unrolled about a metre of fuse from the extra roll that the old man had sold to us at the airstrip that day, and tied it to the end of the shorter fuses that I'd twisted together. I placed the bundle of *bombitas* on top of the only crate that I hadn't doused in gasoline, put everything else back into my backpack and slung it around my shoulders. I walked back to the barn door to peek out at the kitchen window one last time before I went back and lit the fuse. According to the old man, each one of the *bombitas* was the same as half of a stick of dynamite, so what I had ready to go was about the same as two whole sticks. I didn't want to be around when it went off.

I was smiling to myself when I took that peek out of the barn door. This was going to be good, I thought. But the smile on my face disappeared when I looked at the kitchen window across the way. I saw the silhouettes of two men standing near the window: the fat man and the muscular outline of Lieutenant Sánchez. The bad cop was holding on to the kicking and screaming figure of Billy! I saw him reach out with his other arm and slap poor Billy right in the face, hard enough that he stopped trying to get away. I looked over to the driveway and saw the cop car. How did I not hear it pull up?

I had to do something of course, but what? There was no way I could just walk right in there and get Billy out. I knew they'd practically have to kill Billy before he'd tell them our plan, and I was pretty sure they didn't want to leave a bunch of torture marks on him. They needed it to look like he'd drowned in the flood. I stood there, just

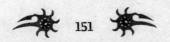

inside the barn with my back to the wall, breathing real hard – the kind of breathing you do when you're scared, and I mean scared witless – trying to figure out a way to save my best friend.

I finally decided that I would create a diversion. The good guys in lots of the books that I'd read would always create a diversion to get the bad guys to look the wrong way or go running in the other direction. If I could get those two out of the farmhouse long enough, I could run in the front door and get Billy the heck out of there before the bad guys knew what had happened. Hopefully we'd get a good enough head start, because we'd just have to make a run for it after that. And then I thought about the cop car out there. How could we outrun someone chasing us down in a car? Then it hit me.

I guessed that the metre-long fuse that I'd put on the bunch of *bombitas* would take about five minutes to burn. I wasn't totally sure, since I was basing it on how fast the fuse had burned that my dad had lit at the Campo Mata Circle at the Fourth of July party. I reached again into my backpack, pulled out another four *bombitas* and quickly went through the same set-up as before, but this time I

didn't tie on any extra fuse. After twisting the four shorter fuses together I figured this bunch of *bombitas* would only burn for about thirty or forty seconds before blowing. I pulled out my lighter and tested it. The flame shot up on the first try, so I knew the flint wasn't wet. For what I had in mind, I'd have to make sure it didn't get wet when I went back into the pouring rain. By now the barn smelled like a gas station with all the fumes from the gasoline I'd poured on everything. I set the second bunch of *bombitas* on the crate next to the first bunch and picked up the end of the long fuse. I took a deep breath and flicked a flame out of the lighter.

'Here goes nothing,' I whispered to nobody but myself.

I lit the end of the fuse, closed the metal case of the lighter, picked up the second bunch of *bombitas* and went over to the barn door for the last time. All three of them were still there in the kitchen. I ran out into the rain and straight over to the back of the cop car. I got down on my hands and knees behind the boot and placed the *bombitas* on the gravel right underneath the fuel tank. Without waiting a second longer than I had to, I opened up the lighter and flicked it. There was no spark! I kept flicking, but nothing happened. A minute had passed; only four more until the *bombitas* in the barn went off. I blew on the lighter trying to get any water off the flint, but it wasn't sparking. Another minute passed; if I couldn't light the fuse in the next few seconds, I was gonna have to get Billy out of the house when the barn blew up and just chance it that we could get away from Lieutenant Sánchez in his cop car. Suddenly I got a spark – not enough to light the lighter fluid, but a spark. I was going to have a blister on my thumb from the rough ridges of the wheel that rubbed against the flint, but I kept trying.

Finally, it happened. The flame shot up and I lit the fuse, but I was shocked how fast it started to work its way to the half sticks of dynamite. It was going to go off in about ten seconds, not thirty, so I got out of there in a hurry. I ran down the drive to the front of the house and jumped out of the rain on to the covered porch and past the two sleeping mutts who hadn't moved a muscle since they ate the meat grenades. I tried the handle of the front door and breathed a big sigh of relief that it wasn't locked.

'Four, three, two, one,' I counted under my breath.

Boom! The *bombitas* under the car went off! A great big flash of light lit up the night sky and it looked like the sun had come out all of a sudden. I could see the banana fields as clear as day and in that flash it looked like all the raindrops had frozen, suspended where they were in the air. In a split second the flash disappeared and a dull red glow replaced it. For sure the car was on fire now. I opened the door and heard shouting coming from the kitchen.

'*Caramba!* What was that?' yelled Guillermo.

'My car!' yelled Sánchez. 'It blew up. Stay here with the kid.'

The screen door opened on its rusty hinges and then slammed back. I ran over to the hallway leading to the kitchen. I saw Guillermo looking out of the window at the fire. He stole a quick glance back at Billy, who was sitting on the breakfast table surrounded by a pyramid of stacked and empty beer bottles, but he didn't see me.

'Stay put, brat,' spat the fat man.

When he looked away again at the fire, I tiptoed down the hall and tried to get Billy's attention by

waving my hand. I could tell that Billy was thinking about making a run for it because he was already looking at the hallway when I waved and he saw me. He took one look at Guillermo's fat back and then did make a run for it, and just when he started Guillermo turned around and saw what was going on.

'Sánchez, the other boy is here in the house!' he yelled through the screen door. 'They're getting away!'

We hightailed it down the hallway and out of the front door. I took a hard right and started running around the house, pretty much in the direction of the place where we rested just before the rain came a-knockin'. We were running across the lawn making a beeline for the banana trees when we saw the muscle-bound Venezuelan cop start out after us. Holy moly, I thought, there was no way we could outrun this guy. He was running at us and was just passing in front of the barn doors when the second blast went off, only this one was even bigger. I'm not sure what else was in that barn, but whatever it was it blew up like a volcano. The doors of the barn flew out, followed by a huge flash of light. One of the doors hit

Sánchez broadside and knocked him down so hard I doubted he'd ever get up again.

We didn't look back to see. We just kept on running into the dark, rainy night.

Chapter 12

The Flood

We were back in El Monte, only this was a part of the jungle that we had never been in before. We knew every trail and pond and tree in the jungle that was close to Campo Mata, but we were on the other side of Pablo Malo's farm, and we had never been here. It didn't help that it was dark and pouring rain.

We weren't running any more, but when we had been I'd bumped up against one of those spiky trees and cut a gash on my right arm. It was stinging and bleeding, but I was way more worried about getting away than I was about a little cut. Billy was right behind me and he was

hurting a bit too. That smack he'd taken on the face from Sánchez had swollen up so much that he could barely see out of his left eye. We hadn't heard or seen anyone coming after us, so I decided to pull out my flashlight and turn it on. Neither one of us had said a word to each other until now.

'Thanks for coming to get me,' said Billy in between pants. 'They were going to drown me and leave my body in the river to rot.'

'Yeah, I know,' I replied. 'I heard 'em too, remember? Pablo Malo's really got it in for us.'

'You know where we are?'

'No idea. But we should run into the river if we keep going this way. Once we get there all we have to do is turn to the right and follow the river to the pump station,' I said. 'Where's Mati?'

'Sánchez kicked him and he ran away. I don't know where he is, but it didn't seem like he got kicked too hard,' replied Billy.

I hoped Sánchez hadn't hurt Mati, but I knew that dog could take care of himself in El Monte.

'You think Todd and Gómez made it to the pump house?' asked Billy.

'Pretty sure they did,' I replied. 'Otherwise they'd have been rounded up like you were. 'Course, they coulda just drowned them in the river right there and thrown their dead bodies in the current.'

Billy stopped walking behind me, so I turned around to look at him. I guess what I'd said didn't meet with his approval 'cos when I shone the light on his face it was really mad-looking and his eyes were brimming with tears.

'Don't say that!' he yelled. 'They're alive and you know it. That's an awful thing to say.'

I did feel bad about saying that. I was just speaking my mind, but after everything that had gone on, I was starting to feel less hopeful about things working out. Pablo Malo and his banshee dog were still out there, and I had a feeling that it would take a little more than dynamite to put Lieutenant Sánchez out of commission for long.

'Listen, I'm sorry,' I said. 'It's been a long night and I'm starting to get tired and cranky. I'm one hundred per cent sure that they're just fine, and we're going to meet up with them and then we're all going to get back to camp.'

'Well, don't ever say something like that again,' he said as he wiped the tears from his already wet-from-all-the-rain cheeks.

I checked my watch. It was almost three thirty, so we still had another couple of hours of darkness. We had been slowly slogging and splashing our way through the jungle for about an hour when we first heard the roar of the river.

'Wow, it must really be high,' said Billy. 'I've never heard it sound so loud.'

'Me neither,' I replied. 'We need to be super careful and stay away from the banks. The rising water will be tearing away at them and they'll be caving in all over the place.'

'For sure, but there's another good reason to stay away from 'em,' said Billy. 'All the caymans and water snakes will be there too. They don't want to get caught in those currents any more than we do.'

I had totally forgotten about that and Billy was right. I felt kind of stupid for not thinking about it myself. It would be a crying shame for us to have gotten this far only to end up in the bellies of some huge reptiles.

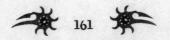

We reached the edge of El Monte and stepped out from the cover of the jungle trees. I shone the flashlight at the river's edge, which was only about ten metres away from us. It was raging and foaming; the milk-chocolate-coloured water was boiling and swirling over huge, rounded boulders. It sounded like a jet taking off. Monster waves crashed again and again into jungle trees that had been uprooted downstream and had wedged here and there between some of the boulders. We watched as the force of the current pushed one of the trees so hard that it cracked the tree right in half and then swept away the two pieces like toothpicks. One of the boulders, the size of a car, moved a little and suddenly started rolling down-river like a bowling ball down an alley, until it crashed into another, bigger boulder and stopped. There were branches and whole bushes every-where, whooshing past us. We could even feel the warmer-than-the-rainwater spray from the crash-ing waves hitting our faces.

I aimed the beam of my flashlight along the banks of the river to the right, in the direction we had to go to get to the pump station. Straight away I saw the greenish white reflections of five

or six pairs of eyes looking right at us and I knew exactly what they were. They were caymans, which are pretty much the same thing as alligators. Seeing them that far off didn't really freak us out. It's when you see one about five metres away that you've got to start worrying. The other eye reflections we had to keep looking for – before we stomped on them, or got too close to them – were anacondas, rabid ocelots and water moccasins. There were other nasty things out there, but those were the ones we were fretting about right then.

'Come on, Billy,' I yelled over the roar of the river. 'We should get about a hundred metres away from the river and then follow it to the pump house. I figure we'll be able to stay away from most of the ornery critters, at least the ones that are waiting on the banks for the drowned animals to come floating by to give 'em a free meal.'

'I'm not too worried 'bout the gators,' he replied. 'It's all the poisonous water snakes that're trying to get away from the river that've got me jumpy.'

Billy and I especially did not like snakes, whether they were the kind to fill you up with

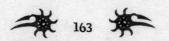

163

enough poison to melt your guts on the inside, or the wrap-around-you-and-squeeze-the-guts-out-of-your-mouth kind. They were a lot harder to see in the dark than gators, and the dark was when they liked to hunt. With gators, you pretty much knew where to look, and that was down. With jungle snakes you had to look down at the ground and up in the tree branches. Never saw a gator drop down out of a tree to get you.

The machete was getting pretty heavy in my hand, but I was sure glad I had it. Not only to protect us from hungry reptiles – which I knew Billy was praying we wouldn't have to use it for – but also because I was having to hack a trail through the thorny bushes and ferns. There were a lot of stands of bamboo too, but we had to go around them because they were way too hard to cut down. We'd come about a mile I guessed, and so far we'd seen a couple of boa constrictors in the branches above us, a long, thin poisonous snake of some kind on the ground and even an ocelot that acted way more scared of us than we were of it. It had stared at us for a minute or so before running away in the other direction.

'How much further d'you figure?' moaned Billy.

164

'I'm getting tired and I surely am hungry enough to eat a whole cow.'

'Should be almost there,' I replied, although I had no clue really.

A minute later I proved to Billy that I was a real jungle man when we stepped out of El Monte and on to the red dirt road. It was the same dirt road that went next to Pablo Malo's farm, only we must have been a couple of miles from the farm. A hundred metres or so off to the left I saw the dark outline of the small cement building that housed the old water pump. I didn't see any light coming from under the door, but I figured that Todd wouldn't want to give away their hideout by turning on his flashlight. The roar of the river was a lot louder now since we weren't surrounded by all the trees and the cover of El Monte.

'I think that we'd better sneak up on the pump house,' I said. 'Might be Pablo Malo's already found them and is in there waiting to ambush us.'

'Good idea.'

We went back into the jungle and started working our way towards the river again until we got right across the road from the building. The rain was starting to ease off a bit and we could see things a

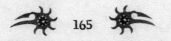

lot clearer than before. Even better, the sun was starting to come out and we could just see the first rays of yellowish light on the rain clouds that were opening up enough for us to see some early morning sky. The storm in the sky was over, but the storm in the river was still going strong.

The pump house didn't have any windows and just one metal door, which was closed. I took my slingshot out and put a ball bearing in the sling. I aimed at the door and let loose a shot. The ball bearing pinged off the door. We waited for about a minute, but nothing happened.

I shot another one at it and then the door opened up. Out came Mati, with his muzzle still on, and he didn't waste any time finding us in our hiding place across the road. He came running over with his tail wagging like mad and whining in that super happy, can't-get-enough-of-your-loving kind of way. We hugged him while he squirmed and jumped around, hopping between Billy and me, making sure that he was getting all of the hugs and pets that we both could give him.

'Mati, good boy. Calm down,' I said. 'Good to see you too.'

About then Todd came out of the building and

when he saw us with Mati he put on a great big grin and started running towards us. We stepped out of the bushes and met him in the middle of the muddy dirt road. He gave me a crushing hug and lifted me off the ground.

'You guys are still alive!' he cried. 'I can't believe it. This is so awesome.'

After he'd about squeezed the life out of me, he let go and hugged Billy like the boa constrictor that we'd been trying to avoid for the last couple of hours.

'What happened to your eye?' said Todd. 'That's a real shiner.'

'Think that's bad?' chuckled Billy. 'You should see the other guy.'

It was right then that we heard the unmistakable sound of Pablo Malo's jeep in the distance – and the sound was getting louder. He was headed our way.

Chapter 13

Showdown at the Pump

From the sound of it, Pablo Malo was just around the next bend. There was no time to get Gómez out of the pump house in time for us all to move into the jungle to hide from him. It probably wouldn't have done us any good anyway – especially if he had Loca with him. I made up my mind then and there. This was my war and mine alone. I was going to finish it now.

'You two grab Mati and get inside the pump house,' I yelled. 'Lock the door from the inside and don't come out until the coast is clear.'

'But –'

'Billy, there's no time to argue. Get in the building now!'

While Todd and Billy scrambled into the pump house with Mati, I ran back to the place where we'd just hidden on the other side of the road. I heard the metal door slam and the latch slide shut. It was all going to be up to me. I was scared to death and shaking like a leaf, but I was sure that I was doing the right thing and I still had one ace up my sleeve. If that didn't work I was going to die, and I doubted that Pablo Malo cared any more how it happened. He'd probably want to torture me. Pablo Malo kind of looked like an Apache, but I hoped he only *looked* like one, because Apaches used to love to tie cowboys down on top of ant hills, then cut open their stomachs and pull out their intestines for the cowboys to see. Then they'd just sit around some place nearby and watch the ants and buzzards eat the guts while the cowboy had to watch too. Then, if the cowboy had been brave while he watched his guts being eaten, they'd go back and scalp him. I was definitely hoping that he wasn't part Apache.

The noise of the old jeep engine suddenly got

169

louder. Pablo Malo had made it around the bend and only had another quarter of a mile or so to the end of the road. There was just one place he was headed to because the collapsed bridge was at the end of the road and the only other thing out here was the pump house. I could see where the bridge had been washed away. There was only about ten metres of it still sticking out over the raging, flooded river. I was betting that the last bit of the bridge would be coming down pretty soon too.

The jeep skidded to a muddy stop right between me and the pump house building. Pablo Malo hopped out of the beat-up truck and then reached back into the cab and pulled out his shotgun. Loca jumped out of the back at the same time and started sniffing around on the ground. Before long Loca had followed the scents around to the other side of the jeep and then started to growl really nasty-like. Pablo Malo laughed out loud and followed Loca around the jeep until he stood right in front of the metal door.

'I know that you are in there, *gringos*,' he yelled at the door. 'Come out and die like men.'

There was no sound from inside the building.

The rain had completely stopped and the sun was now starting to heat up. Since everything was soaked from the rainstorm, the air was heavy with humidity. I was already sweating from fright, but the wet heat was making it worse. My T-shirt stuck to me like glue.

'No? You won't come out?' he yelled. 'Well then, maybe you can cook in that oven for a while. It will be getting much hotter soon, *amigos*. You cook like chickens for dinner. Loca likes her meat cooked.'

Pablo Malo laughed again. He was very pleased with himself, it seemed. I couldn't see him on the other side of the jeep, but I heard the sound of bottles clinking against one another and then the quick hiss of a bottle being opened.

'I will have a few cold beers while I wait for my dinner to cook.'

I heard him chugging his beer. I knew he was doing it as loud as he could so that my trapped friends would hear it. He was probably just as happy – maybe even happier – torturing them to death rather than just getting it over with quickly.

'Ahh . . . a cold beer on a hot morning in El Monte. There is nothing quite like it, *amigos*.

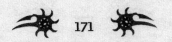

171

Sure you don't want to come out and share one last beer with Pablo?'

He laughed again. He was really enjoying himself. Well, I had had it up to here with his shenanigans. I stepped out of the bushes with my slingshot aimed right at him, my heart almost beating its way out of my chest. Loca heard me first and gave a quick bark before tearing around the jeep at me. She skidded to a stop when she saw the slingshot and started her fangy growling. The fur on her back stood up at about the same time the hair on my neck did. Pablo Malo turned around real casual-like with the shotgun in his right hand and the beer bottle in the other. The smile on his face was not the kind of smile that I had just seen on Todd's face. This one had cold, dark eyes above it. I knew he could see the wild pumping of my heart through my glued-on T-shirt, and I'm sure that made him even happier. He lifted the beer to his lips and took another swig of it without taking his snake eyes off me. He didn't even lift his shotgun to aim it at me.

'So the leader of the Machacas is the only one brave enough to face me,' he sneered. 'What do

you think you will do with that puny rubber band, eh? Maybe kill me like David did with Goliath?'

'You leave us alone or else,' I said. Boy, was that feeble or what?

Pablo Malo's head flung back as he looked up to the sky, laughing really loudly in the way that all the crazed maniac bad guys did in the movies. Only this wasn't a movie, much as I wished it was. I let loose the sling and the ball bearing landed right where I aimed. It went straight into his open, laughing mouth. That shut him up real fast, which was the only good thing that came of it. He dropped his beer bottle and reached up with that hand to cover his mouth. At the same time he pulled up the shotgun and aimed it straight at me. The hand that covered his mouth was now oozing with blood. The blood came dripping out from between his fingers and bright red drops of it fell on to his chest and on the mud at his feet. He stood there staring at me for a long moment with his hand still covering his mouth.

Maybe I couldn't see things clearly because I was so frightened, but it seemed his eyes had changed, like in the movies when vampires' eyes change when they smell blood. Pablo Malo's

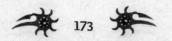

eyes didn't seem human. They were totally dark. It was the scariest thing I had ever seen: the bright red blood, the blackest eyes in the world and the two barrels of his shotgun aimed at my chest. I was about to die and I knew it.

He started to walk slowly towards me with the shotgun aimed straight ahead. He still hadn't said a word. Maybe I had smashed something in his mouth that he needed for talking. Or maybe he figured that the shotgun would be doing the rest of the talking. I took a step backwards for every step he took towards me. We were only ten paces apart, so I knew that he couldn't miss and that they'd be lucky to find hand-sized pieces of me after he pulled the trigger. Another step forward, another step backward. I could hear the roar of the river behind me. I realised what he was planning now, but there was nothing I could do about it. He was going to blow me away into the raging water. They would never know what had happened to me. And when he was done with me, he would repeat the procedure with each one of my friends in the pump house.

Step forward, step back, step forward, step back. I was getting ever closer to the river and

174

even though I knew it from the roar of the water, I glanced over my shoulder to take one last look at my final resting place. I was now at the jagged edge of the bridge, on one side of the road that used to go over the river, and Pablo Malo was on the other side of the road directly across from me. The raging torrent was right there, five metres below where we each stood. I had reached the end of the line. It reminded me of one of those gunfights that I loved reading about in my Louis L'Amour westerns, only I didn't have a gun and no one was going to see who had the fastest draw. Pablo Malo finally took his blood-drenched hand away from his mouth and placed it on the barrel of the shotgun. He put the shotgun to his shoulder and peered down the sight, aiming the barrels straight at my head, like a soldier in a firing squad about to carry out his orders. Only there wasn't going to be a 'ready, aim, fire' this time.

Pablo Malo smiled again and the blood kept dripping from his lips on to his chest. He spat out the pieces of some of his front teeth and they landed on the ground between us. I looked at them, then back up at the black vampire-ghoul-zombie-murderer eyes.

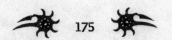

'And now, Avery McShane, you die!'

He pulled the trigger. The finger drew back and I saw what happened next in the slowest motion possible. I saw the tiniest give when the trigger passed the point of no return and that little gear inside let the hammer smash down on the back of the casing of the shotgun shell. I swear that I saw the steel barrel of that shotgun swell a little near where the pellets began their supersonic journey to blow my head off, and I swear I could see that murderous bulge of lead death move down the barrel on its way towards me. And when that packet of pellets hit the rock that I had jammed in that barrel – on that day at the airstrip, the day we bought the *bombitas* – I swear I could see those pellets stop and turn around and head in the opposite direction, in the only other direction they could, in the direction of the path of least resistance. Now, while I cannot be sure that I saw all of that, what I can tell you for sure is that a split second later Pablo Malo's head was gone from his shoulders! The face, the one with the horrible black eyes and the bleeding mouth, was gone! The kickback from that jammed shotgun barrel had blown his head clean off. His headless body didn't move for what seemed an eternity, and then – in real slow motion this time – it fell backward right over the edge of the bridge and disappeared into the chocolate currents of the flooded jungle river.

☀ Chapter 14 ☀

When You Think It Is Safe . . .

I dropped to my hands and knees there, at the edge of the washed-away bridge. My legs had gone to rubber and my heart was pumping the blood in my veins to every place in my body except my head. I was dizzy and nauseated to the point of throwing up, when I remembered about Loca. That cleared my mind real quick. I looked to where she'd been growling at me during the death march I'd taken with Pablo Malo, but she wasn't there.

I didn't waste any time getting back up on my feet or putting a new ball bearing in my slingshot. Loca wasn't over by the jeep or next to the pump

house. She was standing at the exact spot where Pablo Malo had been standing before he lost his head, and she was looking down at the river where his body had fallen. She barked a question at the river, but it didn't answer her; it just kept on roaring past us. I actually felt kind of sorry for her right about then, but when she turned around and looked at me, I went back to just being plain scared witless about what she'd be trying to do to me for killing Pablo. I pulled back on the slingshot and took careful aim at her. I expected her to snarl, to show me her huge fangs, but she didn't. Instead she just looked at me with a confused expression and barked at me once, just like she had at the river.

'He's gone, Loca,' I said.

She cocked her head when I told her that, as if she knew what I meant, and glanced one more time at the river. Then she just turned and walked away into El Monte. She was headed downstream, so I figured that she was going to go and find her master and, knowing Loca, she wasn't going to stop searching until she found him.

I knocked on the metal door of the pump house. It was our super-secret Machaca knock.

'You guys can come out now,' I yelled. 'The coast is clear.'

It took them a full minute to respond. I could hear them whispering to each other inside.

'How do we know that Pablo Malo hasn't got a gun to your head?' came the reply. It was Billy's voice. 'Maybe he's making you trick us into coming out.'

'Guys, Pablo Malo's not going to be shooting anybody ever again,' I said. 'He's on a one way trip down the river to the ocean.'

I heard the latch slide back and the door opened. First one out was Mati and he didn't have his muzzle on any more. He jumped up on me, planted his front paws on my chest and started licking my face like I'd just rubbed dog food all over it. Next one out was Todd and he came over without saying a word and gave me a great big bear hug. I looked over his shoulder while he was squeezing the air out of my lungs and saw Billy come out. He had been crying and the tears were still on his cheeks. He didn't walk over to me, but just stood there looking at me. Todd unwrapped his bear arms and stood off to the side, watching Billy and me look at each other.

'Avery McShane,' said Billy, 'don't ever do something like that again. We're best friends and we're Machacas. We stick together through thick and thin.'

'Billy, I'm sorry,' I replied. 'It was the only way I could see this thing play out.'

I walked over to Billy and when I put my arms around him he started to bawl like a little baby, and I did a little crying too.

'I thought you were dead,' sniffed Billy. 'When that shotgun went off . . .'

'I know, I'm sorry,' I replied. 'But it's all over now and no one else is going to die today.'

Todd and I helped Capitán Gómez out of the pump house and we had to work extra hard to get him into the driver's seat of the jeep. He was wincing and groaning, and you just knew that he'd be holed up in the clinic for a while. Once he was in the front seat, he scooted around until he got as comfortable as he could. Then he looked over at me and managed a smile.

'Señor McShane Junior, you are one brave *gringo*,' he said. 'You must tell me what has happened.'

So I told him. Billy already knew most of the story and he kept interrupting with comments

like 'it was a huge ball of fire' and 'caymans all over the place'. Todd looked at me like I was a real-life G.I. Joe, and come to think of it, I guess I would've made that soldier real proud if he'd known what I'd done. I told Gómez about the *bombitas*, jamming the stones into the barrels of the shotgun and blowing up Pablo Malo's farm. The Venezuelan police chief smiled weakly, even though I'm pretty sure it hurt to do it. In the sunlight it was easier to see how beat-up he really was, though his cuts and gashes had stopped bleeding and were starting to scab over.

'So that's about it,' I said.

'That it is quite a story,' replied Gómez. 'I am sure that your parents will be proud of you.'

When he said that, Billy and Todd and I looked at each other, and then I looked back at Gómez.

'We don't think that they should know what happened,' I said. 'You promised us that you wouldn't tell them unless you really had to.'

'That is true, Avery,' he replied, 'but I have no proof of the smuggling operation and we still do not know who killed Gustavo Muñoz. I will need you to testify at least about the diamond business and Guillermo Santos's part in the operation.'

Well, I guess that I hadn't told the *whole* story.

'Hold on a second,' I said. 'I'll be right back.'

I walked over to my hiding place across the dirt road from the jeep, picked up my backpack and machete and brought them to the jeep. I threw the machete in the back and placed the backpack on the passenger seat. I rummaged around in the pack, pulled out my camera and handed it to Capitán Gómez.

'I took a bunch of photos of the inside of the barn,' I said. 'I'm hoping they might be proof enough about the whole operation.'

Capitán Gómez took the camera and then looked at me, still smiling. He looked at the photos on the camera's screen.

'These should do the trick,' said the police chief.

I suddenly remembered the diamonds in my pocket. I handed him the small pouch and he poured a few of the sparkling gems on to his palm. He looked up at me.

'Quite the detective, aren't you,' he said with a twinkle in his eyes.

'So you won't need to tell our parents about all this, right?' I said. 'I mean, now that you have all of this evidence.'

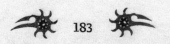

The Capitán laughed and then winced from it. The pain made his smile go away for a moment and then it came back.

'I will do my best, but I cannot promise you,' he said. 'I may still need your testimony once we find out who killed the young man you boys saw at the clinic.'

'My money's on Sánchez,' said Billy. 'Pablo Malo would have used his shotgun, and Sánchez had those pistols. The dead guy had bullet holes in him.'

'Let's get you boys back home,' said the Capitán, reaching for the keys in the ignition.

'Umm, are you OK to drive? My dad's let me take the wheel a couple of times,' said Todd hopefully.

Capitán Gómez managed another smile.

'I think I can make it to the clinic,' he said. 'I will have the doctor there call the Policía Nacional in Anaco and have them send some officers to the farmhouse.'

I didn't say anything, but it worried me. It would take those officers several hours to make the trip from Anaco to Campo Mata. My dad and I had taken the same trip lots of times to play in golf tournaments there. By the time the police got

184

there, Sánchez and Guillermo might be long gone – and they knew where each one of us lived.

'They could be long gone by the time the officers get there,' I said.

'I know,' sighed Gómez, 'but I am in no shape to handle them, and you three have already been through enough. It's the best I can do under the circumstances.'

He was right about one thing. He needed to get to the clinic. I wasn't so sure about the other. We'd been through hell and back, but there were still some loose ends and I didn't want any of them to come after us. I made up my mind right then and there, but I didn't want the Capitán to know what I was thinking. I didn't even want Billy and Todd to know.

'OK,' I said. 'We'd better get going.'

Capitán Gómez turned the key and the old jeep engine coughed and sputtered its way back to life. I leaped into the passenger seat and Mati jumped on to my lap. Billy and Todd hopped into the back with the backpacks and machetes. Gómez put it in gear and we started bouncing and splashing our way down the muddy dirt road.

When we had gone about a mile down the road I turned to Gómez.

'Do you think that you can make it to the police station on your own?' I yelled over the noise of the engine.

The man's face was pale and his jaw tensed with every pothole the jeep hit.

'It is painful,' he said, 'but yes, I can make it.'

'Good,' I said. 'You think you could drop us off at the path to the mango tree? We sure don't want anyone to see us in this jeep. We'll go to the tree house, wait a little while, then head on home and act like nothing ever happened.'

The police chief kept on driving while he thought about it.

'OK,' he said. 'I will drop you off there, but go straight home. Do not linger at the tree house.'

'It's a deal,' I said, but he didn't see that I had crossed my fingers.

Smoke was still rising from Pablo Malo's place when we passed by the plantation, but we couldn't see what was left of the building through the banana trees. Capitán Gómez brought the jeep to a stop a

186

hundred metres further down the road, in front of the path that I was pointing at. Mati jumped out on to the dirt road, followed by the rest of us Machacas.

'Now remember,' said Capitán Gómez, 'straight home, OK?'

'OK,' I said.

Billy and Todd nodded in agreement.

'You must promise,' he insisted.

'I promise,' I said, with my fingers firmly crossed behind my back.

'Good,' said the officer. 'I must be going, but I will need to talk to you boys later.'

'We'll drop by the clinic later today to check in on you,' I said.

Capitán Gómez put the car into gear and was about to pull away when he turned once more to face us.

'Thank you,' he said. 'For saving my life.'

And then he drove away.

I turned to see Billy and Todd with their hands on their hips and scowls on their faces.

'What?' I said.

'You had your fingers crossed when you promised him we'd be going home,' said Billy. 'I saw it.'

'You're not going straight home, are you?' said Todd. 'You're thinking of going back to the farm, right?'

It was true. I just couldn't stand the thought that Sánchez and Santos might get away, after all they'd done. I didn't want to think that they might be hiding in El Monte, waiting to get back at us.

'You two don't have to go,' I said.

'You're nuts,' whined Billy. 'We finally get away and you want to go back?'

'That's Capitán Gómez's problem now,' said Todd. 'Let the police handle it.'

'You guys get going,' I said. 'I'll meet you at the clinic, say just after lunch?'

All I had was my machete and Mati, which wasn't much compared to Lieutenant Sánchez's pistols, but it was going to have to do. I was scared, for sure, but I figured I didn't want to live my life always looking over my shoulder to see if they were about to jump me.

'Oh, and I'll need that rope,' I said to Todd, pointing at his backpack.

He reached into his pack and handed me the coil of rope.

'What're you going to do with this?' he said.

'Tie Sánchez up,' I replied. 'If he's still under the barn door . . . if he's still alive.'

'If he's alive,' said Billy, 'he'll probably use it to hang you by the neck from the nearest tree.'

I ignored him.

'Come on, Mati,' I said. 'One last thing to do.'

I was almost at the cattle guard at the entrance when I heard them running up behind me. It made me smile. I turned around and waited for them to catch up. We were Machacas and we were all in this together. I knew they'd come. They stopped in front of me, breathing hard from the short run in the hot sun.

'All right,' panted Billy, 'let's get this over with.'

'Yeah,' said Todd, 'but I think we oughta sneak up on the place instead of just walking right up the road.'

'Good idea,' I said. 'Let's do that and see what's going on.'

We were sneaking up through the rows of banana trees along the edge of the narrow gravel road, when I saw a nice ripe bunch of bananas. Billy and Todd saw it too, but none of us mentioned it. What was there to say? We knew that if we had

189

seen that yellow bunch of bananas that day when we first came sneaking in, we'd have grabbed it and run out of there. None of what happened after would have taken place.

The farmhouse came into view and we could also see the barn, or what was left of it. The roof was completely gone and the only things standing were three blackened walls. They looked like the crumbling walls of an old abandoned Spanish mission. The metal skeleton of Lieutenant Sánchez's burned-out cop car was still giving off a little bit of oily smoke, but not nearly as much smoke as the barn. I saw that some of the wooden beams from the rafters had fallen down inside and still had flames coming off them.

As we came around the side of the house I saw the big, thick barn door that had blown off its hinges lying flat on the ground about halfway between the house and the burning barn. It wasn't completely flat though and that was because Sánchez was still under it. I saw his feet sticking out from under it, like the Wicked Witch's in *The Wizard of Oz* after Dorothy's house fell on her. Only these weren't ruby slippers. These were black boots.

'Looks like Sánchez is still out for the count,' I whispered.

'Or dead,' whispered Todd.

'Or playing possum, just waiting for us to get close enough to shoot us to smithereens,' whispered Billy.

I had my machete tight in my right hand, and Billy and Todd each had their slingshots loaded. They followed me around to the front of the house and up the porch steps to the open door. The two mutts were still there on the porch all curled up, and I was afraid that we'd overdosed them with too much sleeping powder.

'They're still breathing,' whispered Billy, who was reading my mind, I guess.

I peered into the room. Nothing had changed. The unused furniture piled up on one side, the radio equipment and the silver spurs – everything was just as when we had first seen it. I crept into the room and over to the hallway leading to the kitchen. We hadn't heard anything yet, but we did when we started to get closer to the kitchen. Someone was snoring loudly, like a rumbling volcano about to erupt. I poked my head around the doorway and saw Guillermo

Santos lying face down on the pink linoleum floor. There were even more empty beer bottles around than I remembered seeing the last time I was there, and most of them were scattered around the fat man. He was totally passed out.

'Guess he figured he'd be going to jail,' said Todd. 'Wanted to get drunk for the last time.'

'That,' said Billy, 'or Pablo Malo told him to stay until he got back from killing us.'

We tied his hands and legs just in case he woke up, and went out through the squeaky screen door. Not even the rusty screech it made when we opened it or the loud slam when it closed behind us was going to wake up Guillermo. I walked across the lawn to where Sánchez's feet stuck out from beneath the heavy wooden door. I pulled out the rope, cut off a long section with my pocket knife and started to tie the man's feet together.

'Hurry up,' hissed Billy.

When I was done, I stood up and kicked one of the black boots, but nothing happened. I kicked it again, this time a lot harder. If he was awake he'd have groaned for sure. Of course, if he had been sleeping it would probably have woken him up. But there was no movement, no painful groans.

'OK, guys,' I said, 'let's lift this thing off him and see what we've got.'

Billy and I got on one side, and Todd handled the other all by himself.

'One, two, three, go,' I counted.

'Use your legs, not your backs,' grunted Billy.

With a whole lot of straining and complaining we managed to get the door a little way off the ground, walk it away from the body and drop it. We looked over at the face-up, squished body of Lieutenant Sánchez. I could tell that one of his legs was broken just below the knee because shins don't normally bend like his was. His right arm was probably broken too. It was all twisted up underneath him at a totally wrong angle. His face was the worst part of it though. The Venezuelan maids back at camp weren't going to think he was so good-looking any more. That's 'cos his nose was practically ripped off and hanging by a thin piece of skin, and one of his ears was missing.

'He's still breathing,' said Billy, pointing at his chest. Seems Billy had become an expert on telling if someone was still breathing.

That got me a little worried, so I moved over

193

next to the body, knelt down, quickly took the one gun he still had out of his holster and handed it to Billy.

'Keep that thing pointed at his chest,' I said. 'He moves, shoot him.'

With the pistol in his hand, Billy was once more the brave western gunfighter.

'You got it,' he said. 'Let's just see him try something.'

I looked at the gun in his hand. It was shaking. He was being brave, but he was terrified of course. I was too.

'You might want to click off the safety first,' I said as I knelt down next to Sánchez.

When I heard the click, I rolled Sánchez on to his stomach and tied his hands behind his back as tightly and as quickly as I could with the rest of the rope. It was kind of gross when I heard his broken arm crack again, but I got it done. I was scared to death while I was doing it that he'd all of a sudden come around and try to strangle me. I finished the job and breathed a big sigh of relief.

Todd had seen the other pistol across the yard near the screen door and was walking over to pick it up from where it must have landed after being

blown out of Sánchez's hand. Billy stood over me, watching Todd hold the other pistol in the palms of his hands like it was going to bite him. And then, just as I was about to stand up, Sánchez suddenly opened his eyes and looked right at me. I froze. I wanted to run away, but couldn't.

'Avery McShane,' he whispered, so low that I was the only one who could hear him. It was a whisper that came half from his mouth and half through where his nose used to be. 'I will find you. Some day, when you think it is safe, I will find you and when I do, I will kill you . . .'

☀ Chapter 15 ☀

The Legend of Loca

It was the tenth of July, my birthday. My parents had set up the tiki torches and picnic tables in the grassy field behind our house, like they did for the Fourth of July party, only there were a lot fewer of them. Almost all of the kids in Campo Mata had been invited, except for Scott and Chris. Everyone would be showing up when the sun started turning orange again on the horizon, but Billy and Todd had asked me to meet them at the hideout a couple of hours before the party started and I was on my way there.

I followed Mati through the gap in the barbed wire fence and walked the short distance to the edge of El Monte. As usual, we both got that feeling that something was going to happen, because something always did when we went into the jungle. Like most days in that part of the world it was steamy and the sky was light blue without a single cloud. We stepped into the cooler, wetter, still air hiding in the shadows of the tropical forest. The sky reminded us it was up there by shooting sharp beams of light through a few gaps in the leaves above us.

We had only taken a few steps down the hard-packed dirt path to the tree house when Stupid Monkey saw us and started fussing again. He was really going at it this time. I figured he was in a bad mood because he still hadn't recovered from staying up all night listening to the ruckus we had caused at Pablo Malo's farm. Seemed to me that he had gotten up on the wrong side of his tree branch every morning since. We took a short cut away from the path through the ferns and toadstools that grew up through the mat of rotting leaves carpeting the damp ground. Stupid Monkey saw what we were doing to get around him and he was having none of it. He started screaming and jumping from branch to branch,

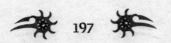

chasing after us, so we had to run for a little while to get out of his poop-tossing range.

We made it to the hideout before the rest of the Machacas. I checked on the threat threads, happy to find them all strung out across the six paths leading to the mango tree. Mati curled up in a tight comfortable ball at the base of the tree and I climbed up the trunk into the room of our tree house.

Everything was back to normal. The stacks of comic books were in the far corner, but the piles were a little taller than before due to all the tape we had used to repair the torn pages. The holsters were back hanging on the nails in the wall just above the comic books. We had dug them up from their graves in the dirt because we knew that the hideout wouldn't be the same without them. We spent a lot of time stitching the belts back together with twine. We cleaned the mud off the pistols and hammered the barrels back as best we could, but we knew that they'd never shoot straight again. We had even filled some new jars and shoe-boxes with critters we found nearby, but we hadn't found another monster worm yet. I was going to miss that guy.

All of a sudden Mati let out a single sharp bark to warn me that someone was out there and, since I was still jumpy after everything that had happened over the last week, I peeked out of the window sort of cautious-like. In my imagination I could picture the headless body of Pablo Malo shuffling out of the bamboo stand, dripping blood from his stump of a neck with his arms straight out feeling around for my neck to throttle, or maybe the noseless and earless face of Sánchez looking up at me in triumph, all ready to follow through with his promise to kill me. But it wasn't either one of them. Instead Billy and Todd came through the bamboo thicket, and they weren't running from someone with a shotgun or a rabid, frothing, banshee dog. They were laughing about some private joke that I wasn't a part of, though I suspected I might have been the butt of it.

'Ahoy the fort,' yelled Billy. 'We come in peace.'

'And bearing gifts for the birthday boy,' chimed in Todd, who was carrying a shoebox under his thick arm.

Todd sat cross-legged on the floor, scratching at the little scabs on the backs of his legs from

when he got shot with the rock salt. Billy was next to him flipping through the unripped pages of a brand new issue of *Iron Man* that had come in the mail. He had a big black-and-blue shiner around his left eye, but the swelling had gone down. They had set the shoebox with my birthday gift on the floor in front of where I was sitting, and were acting all casual and offhand-ish.

'So do you want me to open it now?' I said. 'Or wait until I open all the presents at the party?'

'Oh, whatever you want,' said Billy without looking up from *Iron Man*.

'Up to you,' said Todd. He was looking at the scab he'd just picked, and I knew he was trying to decide whether to eat it or not. It was salted, so it would probably taste better than most.

'OK, I'll just open it up now,' I said.

Neither one of them looked up when I reached out to pull the top off the shoebox. I hesitated a moment. Something was up, I thought. They were acting pretty strange. But my curiosity got the better of me, so I went on ahead and opened up the box. When I saw it I let out a good imitation of one of Billy's girly screams,

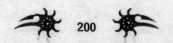

and it was exactly what they'd hoped for. All of a sudden they were laughing like crazy and congratulating each other. That's because the first thing I saw in the box was a snake with dark black eyes and sharp fangs all coiled up and ready to sink its poisonous fangs into my hand. I had already jumped back and scrambled away like a madman to get away from the killer reptile, when I realised that the snake looked a little odd. My buddies were laughing so hard that they both had tears running down their cheeks. I looked back into the box, this time from a safe distance, and saw what they'd done. It wasn't a snake at all. It was one of those monster worms and they had painted on eyes and a mouth with a magic marker, and had glued on two small fang-shaped pieces of paper coming out of the fake mouth. They'd even gone so far as to draw in a little red at the tips of the fangs to make it look like blood.

Now it was my turn to laugh. They had gotten me fair and square.

'Oh, now *that* was a good one,' I said. 'I should've known you guys wouldn't get near a real snake, much less put it in a shoebox.'

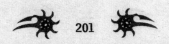

'It was hard to paint it up,' laughed Billy. 'It kept squirming.'

'There's more,' said Todd, wiping the tears from his cheeks. 'Check it out.'

First thing I did was put the worm snake in an empty cardboard box. We'd fix up something for him later, with dirt in it, like we had for the first one. I looked back in the box, a little more cautiously this time, to see what else they had in store for me. The next gift was especially cool. It was the pair of silver spurs that the gang had taken from the dead guy on the concrete slab.

'Capitán Gómez gave us permission,' said Billy. 'He said that the dead guy would have wanted to give them to you for solving the mystery of how he got killed.'

Turns out that Gustavo Muñoz, the dead guy, was killed by Lieutenant Sánchez. Gustavo had been out in El Monte riding his horse around, and when he saw the farmhouse he decided to go and see if he could get a job there and make a little spare change before the annual cattle round-up. When no one answered the front door he had gone around the back to the barn because he'd heard the sounds of a saw coming

from inside it. With all the noise from the sawing, Pablo Malo hadn't heard Muñoz walk up. But Muñoz had seen Malo pulling out the little sacks of diamonds and pretty quickly put the pieces together. He skedaddled out of there straight to the police station in Campo Mata. Problem was that Lieutenant Sánchez was the first person he saw when he got there. Sánchez got Muñoz to go back with him to the farmhouse and that's where he shot him. We knew all of this because Guillermo Santos had sung like a bird after he woke up in jail. With Sánchez under guard in the clinic and Pablo Malo dead, the fat man didn't have to worry about what they'd do to him. He told the police everything.

'Thanks, guys,' I said. 'I think we should keep them here at the hideout. I'll hammer in a nail by the holsters and hang these next to them.'

The last thing in the shoebox was a worn-out, dog-eared *Mad* magazine. It was only one, and it wouldn't replace all the others Pablo Malo had stolen from us, but it was a start and it made me feel like everything would soon be back to normal at the tree house.

'These are the best gifts,' I said.

I slid the magazine under my stack of *Thor* comic books.

'Hey, guess what I found out?' I said. 'Turns out there's a big cayman in Mata Pond.'

'No way,' replied a worried Billy. 'You're just joshing us.'

'Nope, Dad saw it when he was looking for his golf ball on number eight. It came after him, so my dad had to take a drop ball, and Mr Slater ended up winning their match by one stroke. Beat my dad for the first time ever.'

'Holy bat caves!' cried Billy. 'You mean we've been swimming in there and pulling out golf balls for years, and there's been a gator there the whole time?'

'Yep, it's a fact.'

The sun was just starting to set on the horizon, and the lighting from the tiki torches was taking over from the disappearing sunlight. Most everybody was there now at the party. My girlfriend Denise was sitting at the picnic table next to mine talking to her twin sister. They looked over

at me sitting by myself and Cathy whispered something in Denise's ear and they both started giggling. Whatever was so funny obviously had to do with me. I tried not to turn red-faced, but I was never any good at hiding a blush, at least not when it came to girls.

Todd was over at the barbecue pit standing next to my dad, who was turning over hamburgers and hot dogs with a big pair of tongs. When my dad wasn't looking Todd snatched up one of those hot dogs and ran away, tossing the burning hot wiener from one hand to the other to keep from singeing himself. Mati ran after him, barking out his demand for a piece of the action. Billy had gone back into the house to change the music, and there wasn't much suspense about which song he was going to put on. Sure enough it was Tex Ritter, every young cowboy's favourite singer. The sounds of *Blood on the Saddle* poured out of the open doors and window of the house. It was a sad song about a cowboy who gets shot in a gunfight and dies, and it made me think again about that gaucho that Sánchez had killed. He had looked like a nice guy, someone I would have gotten along with just fine. He had been in the

wrong place at the wrong time, just like a cowboy on a cattle drive getting caught in a sudden stampede and trampled to a pulp.

I saw Nelly walking over to my table with a plate full of food she'd put together for me. She had come back the day before from her time off, and while she still wasn't herself, she did seem a mite better than last week. At least she was talking to me instead of throwing hot pans into the sink and crying all the time. She came up beside me and set the paper plate on the table in front of me.

'*Gracias*, Nelly,' I said. 'I surely am hungry.'

'*De nada*,' she replied.

Instead of walking away, she just stood there next to me, looking me straight in the eye. To my horror I saw her eyes fill up with tears and then they started to drip down her cheeks. Oh no, I thought, not again. What is it with grown-ups?

'*Gracias*, Avery,' she said in Spanish, 'for catching the man who killed my brother.'

Her brother? Gustavo Muñoz was her brother? Was that what my parents didn't want to tell me?

Well, that certainly explained a lot – at least about her crying and all – but it didn't help me

figure out what to say next. I hadn't told anyone what happened at Pablo Malo's farm, most especially Mom and Dad. We had each gone home that morning as if nothing had happened, as if we'd just gotten tired of spending the night at each other's houses. For sure my parents asked me why I had scratches on my arms and why my clothes were so muddy and wet, but I told them that we'd been out in El Monte, which was not technically speaking a lie. Far as I could tell they believed me, because I didn't get grounded. And neither did Billy or Todd. Billy's parents fussed a bit about his shiner and swollen eye, and they threatened to keep him away from Todd, who they suspected of being the one who had smacked him. But the dust cleared soon enough and everything had gone back to normal.

'Capitán Gómez told me everything that you did,' continued Nelly. 'That the *policía* from Anaco found my brother's murderer tied up and his guns on the kitchen counter. He said that you are a hero and very brave.'

I started blushing again, but I still couldn't get a word out. Nelly smiled at me through her tears.

'He asked me if Billy and Todd could give you my brother's silver spurs,' she went on, 'and I told him they could. You will think about him when you look at them, yes? He was a good man, a good gaucho and the best brother in the world.'

The words finally started to come out.

'I'm so sorry that your brother died, Nelly,' I said. 'Thank you for giving me his spurs. Every time I look at them I'll think about your brother, about him up there somewhere riding horses and rounding up cattle.'

'He is with God in heaven,' she said.

Nelly walked away and I never heard her talk about her brother again. I sat there alone just staring at my food. It was a funny thing, but I was starting to understand why people of different ages cry about different things. When you're young you cry if someone takes your toy or when you fall and scrape your knee, but adults don't often cry about those kinds of things. An adult cries when someone close to them dies, which I was starting to understand, or when someone gives them something, which I still didn't totally understand. So I figured that I must have been getting close to becoming an adult because I knew that I would feel sad for Nelly every time I saw those silver spurs, and that I might even cry.

The party was over and there was only one tiki torch still lit in the grassy field behind my house, and that's where I was. I had promised Mom that I'd be coming in soon, but I just wanted to sit in the fresh air for a bit before calling it a night. The stars were out and I saw Venus and Mars and Orion's Belt. The half-moon was low on the horizon, on its way to take a dip in the distant Pacific Ocean with the sun. I looked out across the field and saw the bumpy black outline of the tops of the tall trees of El Monte against the background of the dark blue sky. I looked down below the treetops and saw the faint outline of the barbed wire fence dimly lit by the yellow light of the solitary tiki torch that I was sitting under. It took me a long moment to accept what I saw next.

She was there, at the edge of the jungle, where the path to the hideout began. Loca stood there,

a motionless ghost in the night, her red eyes boring into mine. I blinked to clear the apparition from my mind, and when I opened my eyes again, she was gone.

THE END

If you loved Avery's awesome adventure,
don't let it stop here!

Visit **www.averymcshane.blogspot.com**
for more on Avery and the gang!

Get to know Greg with this cool Q & A

Who is your favourite villain in a book?
Long John Silver, of course. He made *Treasure Island* click. Likeable and murderous at the same time – I liked him, then I didn't, then I thought maybe he'd come around, and then he didn't.

If you could be a character from a book who would you be?
This is cheating, because the novelization came after the movies, but I would be Indiana Jones. I haven't even read the books, but I know from the movies that he's who I'd want to be. I know for a fact that if I had it to do all over again, I'd be an archaeologist and I'd explore for things in remote places where adventures were bound to happen.

If you could recommend just one book for everyone to read what would it be?
That is a tough one. If just one, for people of any age, I would have to go with *The Lord of the Rings*.